Ian Joseph writes fast-moving, fantastical adventure stories about the Spark children – Jammy Jimmy, Awesome Annie and Magic Mazik – for his grandchildren, encouraging them to be fun-loving, bold and rebellious. He thought he would share them with you – the stories, not the grandchildren – and hopes you will enjoy reading them as much as he loved writing them, whatever your age.

In Parvo Magnus
In small things, greatness

The Fantastical Adventure of

Magic Mazik

IAN JOSEPH

ILLUSTRATED BY AMY LEVENE

Available from

www.ypdbooks.com

and

www.mazikspark.com

A CIP catalogue record for this book is available from the British Library.

ISBN 978-1-8384652-0-9

Book layout and design by Clare Brayshaw

Illustrations © Amy Levene

Prepared and printed by:

York Publishing Services Ltd
64 Hallfield Road
Layerthorpe
York YO31 7ZQ

Tel: 01904 431213

Website: www.yps-publishing.co.uk

Contents

Acknowledgements

My thanks to Amy Levene not only for her inventive illustrations, which so enrich the text, but also for her helpful suggestions. Not least of these was introducing me to Matthew Bellwood, who has been a long-sought and inspirational mentor – an alchemist.

My gratitude to all who have encouraged me in this endeavour.

Maz·ik (măz-ĭk)
Noun: A mischievous child.

Obadiah Spark's Family Tree

(Obadiah Sparks all the way to the top)

Obadiah Spark

↓

Obadiah Spark

↓

Obadiah Spark

↓

Gramps Obadiah Spark m. Grandma Lucy

↓

George Spark (dec'd) m. Amy

↓

Jammy Jimmy   Awesome Annie   Magic Mazik

Chapter 1

Big Brother

Even when it was not playing around the mouth in his freckle-fresh face, Mazik's smile would still sparkle in his jet-black eyes. Only rarely did it fade. But now, quite unexpectedly, a nagging worry dimmed his expression. He struggled to understand it. This was Jimmy's big moment: the grown brother he hero-worshipped; Jimmy, on the main stage at the university he had founded, in front of a global audience, being interviewed about *Jammy Jimmy,* the book about his many fantastic achievements.

The feeling wasn't anger. It couldn't be disappointment, certainly not with Jimmy. Disappointment with himself? That didn't feel quite right. No, in his mind the worry had a green tone. Green for envy.

He was jealous!

This stark thought struck him hard. He hated feeling so negatively about his adored brother. Why ever was he?

After a moment it dawned on him. *Just the usual, I guess: sibling rivalry*

~

Detective Chief Inspector Vera Smidgley was in charge of security. To some people, DCI Smidgley seemed like a rather gruff woman. Certainly, she was stressed and scruffy. Her frizzy hair hadn't been near a brush for some considerable time and she badly needed a fortnight's holiday or early retirement. But looks were deceiving. Her razor-sharp mind was on higher matters. Despite being hardened by the job, she had a heart of gold and a soft spot for the Sparks, given all the times she'd enjoyed – yes, that was the word – *enjoyed* sorting out their life-threatening escapades.

She bustled around worrying about last minute arrangements, struggling to keep the mob of reporters and photographers at bay. She was particularly anxious about the temporary display case in the foyer, exhibiting Jimmy's priceless Moon rocks and asteroid samples; she'd be hugely relieved when Jimmy packed it up and took it home.

At last, the lights were dimmed and the interviewer – the head of High Woodley's

International Novation University, INU for short – walked confidently onto the stage.

'Ladies and Gentlemen, it gives me the greatest pleasure to introduce...' She paused, then raised her voice dramatically, '...Dr James Spark!'

To loud applause, Jimmy strolled across the stage, waving and smiling confidently. Jimmy shared Mazik's easy smile, smooth complexion and freckles, but with spiky red hair. They both sat down and checked their microphones.

'Dr Spark – Jimmy – you've achieved so much at such a young age, it's hard to know where to start.'

Jimmy smiled graciously. Mazik was sitting in the reserved seats in the front row, between his mid-teen sister, Annie and his often-absent mother, Amy. Her husband, George, had been killed in a hit-and-run motor incident when she was pregnant with Mazik. She buried him in grief and herself in graft.

George's father, Obadiah Spark, known to all as 'Gramps', was a wily old Yorkshire archaeologist, short in height and temperament but with a constant, humorous twinkle in his eye. He'd clung on to a strong accent and his old flat cap. He was devoted to his grandchildren, indeed a father figure to them, particularly for Mazik.

The interviewer continued: 'You were born and bred here in High Woodley.'

'And proudly so. It's given me everything I've ever wanted,' answered the youthful Jimmy. He beamed knowingly at his childhood sweetheart, Harmony, who was sitting next to Annie. As Mazik listened, he again felt that twinge of anguish and a frown briefly wrinkled his brow.

'I know I should keep it for last, but I can't resist asking about your most recent exciting adventure.'

'Ah, the space trip,' laughed Jimmy. 'I was dead for a little while –' There was an intake of breath from the audience '– but I seem to have recovered!' The audience laughed.

That could have been me in space, thought Mazik. *It should have been!*

'Your crew travelled the greatest distance ever from Earth.'

'The journeys out and back didn't involve anything that hadn't been done by others a long time ago,' said Jimmy, with typical modesty.

'But landing on a spinning asteroid was a remarkable achievement, based largely on your mathematical skill.'

'It's not just that it was turning rapidly, but that it was twisting, rotating, rolling and spinning all at the same time.'

'And you were the one that worked out the maths and guided your spacecraft, *Thrymsa*, to a smooth touchdown on the mineral-rich *Paulinus 627*.'

'No, that's crediting me with too much. The captain was our pilot. Mine was just a bit part, really.' Mazik was erupting with envy. *I want to do something like that: be someone. It's hopeless. It's all too difficult.* He tried to focus back on the interview.

'...and that's when the meteorite shower struck?'

'I was with an old friend, the *Thrymsa* navigator. Everything had been going so smoothly. We had to set up some kit at the far end of *Paulinus 627* – the asteroid – and when we were yomping back, I saw this line of little explosions – micro-meteorites smashing into the surface dust – heading straight towards us at incredible speed. They were coming far too fast for us to react. We could so easily have been killed, but – luckily – it was only my breathing tube that was severed.'

'Only!?'

'Had my colleague not been so amazingly fit and strong – he plays rugby sevens in the national squad – he'd have never managed to get me back to the space capsule alive. I flatlined for at least two minutes.' The audience gasped. Mazik was caught between emotions: pride, relief, excitement...but predominantly the lingering guilt of jealousy. *I'm going to be that famous, one day. I don't know how, but I will! I will!*

~

Jimmy went on to describe how the meteorite shower had damaged *Thrymsa's* heat shield, so that they couldn't return to Earth as planned. The craft wouldn't have been able to survive the heat of re-entry. Instead, they had navigated the fabulously valuable asteroid to a soft landing on the Moon. It was here where they'd met the backup craft which had carried them home.

Though it had remained a closely-guarded secret, Mazik knew from Jimmy that during the homeward flight the crew had been contacted by an alien force: an electromagnetic colony of subatomic particles, calling itself *Qua*. Through this contact, *Qua* had accessed the internet and memorized everything.

E v e r y t h i n g!

It was fortunate that *Qua* was a friendly force.

~

The interviewer went back, to when Jimmy was a bit older than Mazik was now and asked him about being a businessman when barely a teenager. He'd teamed up with a very gifted programmer, Dizzy Tech and together they'd made various inventions.

'What was your favourite enterprise?' asked the interviewer.

'Oh, undoubtedly *Rox-On.*'

'That was the rocket-driven delivery system, right?'

'Yeah! Although we had a few problems with that! For the first few deliveries, we hadn't got proper security checks in place. We suddenly realised that one of the first delivery rockets was heading straight for Number 10, Downing Street!'

'Oh, a tad bothersome!'

'A moment of sheer panic! We assumed it had an explosive device on board.'

'Oh, my word! Whatever did you do?'

'I hit the Return to Sender button!' Half the audience erupted in laughter; the other half gasped in horror.

The interviewer decided not to explore that line of enquiry any further, but instead asked, 'What became of *Rox-On*?'

'After that incident, we just wanted to get rid of the whole thing quickly. We sold it in the first week!'

Jimmy went on to explain that a rich, global online retailer, *Notax*, decided *Rox-On* was ideal for most of its huge number of deliveries – over a billion annually, worldwide! They'd paid Jimmy and Dizzy an unimaginably enormous sum to buy it. Jimmy and Dizzy had spent the profits on building *Revolution!* – a community sports centre, on a site next to Folly Park in High Woodley.

While the audience applauded, Mazik fumed. The crease in his forehead had deepened and, for the first time he could remember, he scowled crossly.

Worse still, the list of Jimmy's achievements went on and on. No wonder he was known as 'Jammy Jimmy'. Jimmy had launched INU in which they were now sitting and persuaded his powerful friends to find the money. When Dizzy had become pregnant with twins, she had stood down as Member of Parliament for High Woodley and, though barely old enough to vote, Jimmy had stood and won the by-election to replace her. *Has Mr Perfect ever put a foot wrong?* wondered Mazik.

Jimmy had abruptly resigned after a year. But, before doing so, he had formed a team of researchers at INU to invent *InuSolar* – molecular-coated sheeting which, when unrolled, converted sunlight to electricity. It could be installed anywhere and was now being used throughout the world, to massively reduce the use of fossil fuels.

And then there were the daring escapes from life-threatening disasters...Mazik was in turmoil. Much as he loved Jimmy, he felt it would be impossible to do anything that anybody would ever notice. He couldn't possibly match his big brother's triumphs.

~

'And finally,' said the interviewer, 'What do you consider your most important achievement?'

'That's easy! Except it wasn't my achievement. I was no more than a bystander, really.'

'Explain,' said the interviewer.

'One day, this very, erm...*unusual* chap came to see me and Dizzy. His name was Frederick Ho.' A tidal wave of applause erupted from the audience. 'As you probably know, it was our computer that Frederick used in order to recover a mountain of money, which had been hidden away by international gangsters, dishonest traders and corrupt politicians. Then, he gave it all back to the people.'

'Perhaps you'd like to explain that in a little more detail for some of our younger audience.'

'Of course. Being so close to it, I forget that it's really a bit complicated.' Jimmy arranged his thoughts, then continued, 'Frederick was *very* shy and totally obsessive – a software genius – but he avoided face-to-face conversation.'

'It's not uncommon. Go on.'

'Well, it's probably best to take an example: the Russian President had stolen hundreds of billions of dollars from the Russian state and hidden it away from prying eyes.'

'Especially from the tax man!'

'Correct. And he was far from the only one. What Frederick did was to hack into those secret places, take back the money and ask the citizens what it should be spent on.'

'A velvet revolution! Even though what he did was strictly illegal.'

'Indeed, but sometimes you have to do a little bad for the greater good. Nobody died,' Jimmy paused and a dark cloud seemed to pass over his face, 'except Frederick.' Jimmy choked up and his eyes moistened.

'What happened?' asked the interviewer, sympathetically.

'He was convinced, with good reason, that brutal agents of some of his targets were gunning for him. He left home and walked about ninety miles, in the rain, at night, hiding during the day and neglecting to eat. He collapsed when he got to our offices. He never recovered.'

'A tragic loss for such a revolutionary genius to die so young.'

'The statue we erected at *Revolution!* attracts visitors from around the world.'

I'm so young, thought Mazik, *it'll take years to do anything. Years and years. I'll never succeed like him. I'll be in his shadow for ever: Jimmy Spark's stupid kid brother.*

Annie glanced at Mazik and noticed his scowl. She leaned in. 'Don't worry, Mazik.' She squeezed his hand reassuringly. 'You'll do even better.'

Mazik was confused. 'What? How do you know what I'm thinking?'

'Believe me, I do,' she whispered. 'Call it "female intuition".'

'Female institution? Like a nunnery?' He really was puzzled, now. But she'd returned her attention to listening to the interview and gradually relaxed her grip.

Do better than Jimmy? thought Mazik, as the catalogue of Jimmy's impossible triumphs continued. *I don't think so. The girl's bonkers.*

Chapter 2

Barnsley

The ball bounced off Gramps' shiny, bald head, glanced off the windowsill and caught the rim of Grandma Lucy's eighteenth-century fine china vase – her most valuable and treasured heirloom – which stood on the antique oak chest in the hall. It rocked from side to side, revolved on its base and gyrated in slow motion towards the edge.

Gramps was transfixed, mesmerised by the balletic motion of the world's last remaining porcelain object from the reign of Queen Marmalade III, as he anticipated it shattering into a thousand worthless shards at his feet.

But Mazik had slid down the bannister head-first and launched himself across the hallway. He stretched a hand under the vase and caught it mid-flight, mere centimetres from the ground. He felt rather proud of himself.

'Ee, that were magic, Mazik!' marvelled Gramps. 'But if tha Grandma knew, she'd have yer guts for garters, lad.'

'One point for a head bounce and a bonus point for the catch. I win!'

''Eckers like! Tha can't mek up rules as tha goes along, son!'

'I'm the Rule Maker, Gramps!'

'Who says?'

'The Rule Maker: me!' shouted Mazik. 'Anyway, you could have caught it!'

'Nay, lad, mi left foot's seventy-five years old! Ah'm not so nimble as thee. Anyway, tha lost three points for hittin' Grandma's best vase, so tha loses, young 'un!'

'Aw, Gramps! It's not fair! Invent a game where we don't break stuff.'

'Right, lad, let's be off t'DIY.'

'Be off to die?'

'DIY. Do It Thysen!'

'Why, Gramps?'

'Tha'll see, lad!' Gramps' twinkling eyes were mirrored by Mazik's.

They jumped into Gramps' vintage Bentley and motored down to the local shops.

'Gramps, doesn't this old crate pollute the air? It must be even older than you are!'

'If tha wants to walk home, lad, ah'll drop thee right 'ere!'

'Is it diesel or petrol?'

'Neither, son! It be 'lectric hybrid!'

'But Gramps, they hadn't invented electric cars when this was built.'

'That's where tha's wrong, Mazik. First production cars were 'lectric – back in the 1880s. This one were diesel when ah bought it. Ah got it right cheap, 'cos who wants diesel these days? But then ah had this beautiful vintage Bentley bodywork grafted onto a new 'lectric hybrid chassis and motor. Fully automated. Ah charges it from solar panels on garage roof. Neat, eh? 'Lectric costs nowt!'

Gramps pulled up at the old ironmongers and bought a dozen three-metre lengths of guttering; a variety of junctions; some connectors; and a bag of sponge balls. Gramps slid the gutters neatly through the unused ski flap in the back seat.

Back at home, Gramps started connecting the gutters. They ran up the stairs to the landing, across the landing, up through the loft hatch and then, with a slight rise, they spiralled around the attic. Mazik climbed the loft ladder, holding the balls and then released them one-by-one into the guttering. He watched them spiral around the loft, drop through the hatch and spill out onto the landing carpet.

'Epic fail!' shouted Mazik.

'Design disaster! Clear the area! Hard hats only! Prepare for total rebuild!' shouted Gramps, hanging upside down out of the loft hatch. He eased the gutters' angle of descent out of the attic hatch and was just about to launch another ball.

~

'Hello!'

They hadn't heard the back-door opening. They exchanged anxious glances.

'Hello, Grandma!' shouted Mazik down the stairwell.

'What's all this on the stairs?' replied Grandma from the hallway.

'We were havin' lesson in Do It Thysen, Grandma!' said Gramps, unconvincingly. 'Eh up, Mazik,' he whispered, 'we're in deep do-dos now, lad!'

Grandma had been out walking Mazik's dog, Chepi, a curly-haired, little terrier with bright eyes and a busy tail. Chepi now sprinted up the stairs three at a time, jumped around Mazik excitedly, grabbed a ball in his mouth and rushed down to show Grandma.

'What have I said about playing football in the house? One day, I'll come home from walking the dog and find my best Queen Marmalade vase smashed to pieces!'

Mazik covered his mouth and chuckled cheekily. 'Let's play "shots-in", outside, Gramps.'

'Best clear up first, Mazik.'

Gramps unclipped the length of gutter from the top of the stairs and Mazik rushed back up the attic steps to haul up the top sections before Grandma Lucy discovered the full extent of the game. She refused to climb the attic steps; they were far too rickety.

'What's this guttering doing on the stairs?' she shouted up at them.

'Resting, Grandma!' laughed Mazik, as he slid down the bannister.

'Well, move it. What have you two been up to? I turn my back for two minutes and the house is in chaos! Why do you need guttering in the house?'

'Gutterball, Grandma. You get a point if the ball stays in the gutter all the way down.'

'*You'll* stay in the gutter all the way down! Go and play in the garden! How much have you spent on this rubbish, Obadiah Spark?' she asked, as Gramps came down looking like a little boy caught with his finger in the apple pie.

'But, Grandma!' complained Mazik. 'It's not as dangerous as "You Lose a Life"!'

'Don't tell me!' begged Grandma Lucy.

'That's where you have to hit the other person with the ball.'

'Not in the house, Mazik!'

'Oh, er, no, Grandma, of course not!' laughed Mazik. He skipped out, shouting, 'You're in goals, Gramps!'

By the time Gramps had got his shoes on and gone out, Mazik was standing in the middle of the dahlias, with the ball under his arm, looking guilty. 'It weren't me, Gramps, honest!'

Gramps picked up the broken stems and replanted then in the ground. 'Just be more careful. Tha'll be in right trouble if her indoors discovers tha's flattened the autumn flaarbed.'

'And mind my dahlias!' Grandma Lucy shouted from inside the house. Mazik stifled a giggle.

'It's three-nil, Gramps!'

'But ah've only just come out! Any road, ah'm done for, lad; arthritic feet, tha knows. How about frisby on the rec'?'

'S'boring! What about cricket?'

'We've no balls left since tha blasted 'em all for six!'

'What about the new gutterballs?'

'Oh, aye, good idea! Nip in and get 'em, lad.'

'Right, but I'm not letting Chepi out, or we'll have *dog sog.*'

'Aye, nowt like dog saliva spinnin' off ball to put uz off uz dinner! Right tasty!'

But once Chepi had heard 'Cricket!' there was no stopping him leaping to catch the ball mid-flight and trying to eat it. They retreated to the garage and set up the table football. 'No spinnin' mind!' said Gramps, as Mazik sunk his first goal with a satisfying 'clunk', leaving the midfield line spinning rapidly. 'Ah sez, no spinnin', lad!'

'First to ten, then lunch, Gramps! Hang on, I'll just put my pocket money on a 10–0 victory for Mazik's Magicians. I'll call Phoney Bet.'

'Tha's nowt left, son. Tha spent it all on them daft football cards. Ah'll give thee a memory test on tha cards, when ah've thrashed thee at table footie!'

Thunk! 'Two-nil, Gramps!'

Swizz...thunk...phew

Mazik and Gramps went outside, took in the view, then looked at each other in amazement. Sitting on the lawn before them was a gleaming spaceship, hissing gently.

'Gramps, is it from outer space?' whispered Mazik.

''Appen it's from back of beyond. Likely Barnsley.'

'Is that in outer space?'

'Some would say so.'

'Should we knock on the door?'

'Ah don't rightly see no doorknocker, lad.'

'Hello!' shouted Mazik. 'Is there anybody in?'

Swizz...phew

A hatch opened at the top of the spacecraft and a head popped up. It was looking away from them, unless it had a *very* hairy face.

Gramps coughed and the head turned. It belonged to an eager-looking young man with a glowing, electric-blue complexion. 'Oh, hello!' he said. 'I'm Captain...Barnsley.' He had overheard Gramps and decided, on the spur of the moment, to adopt the name. 'Er...Yorke Barnsley.'

'Is tha lost, lad? This is neither York nor Barnsley!'

'That's my name: Yorke Barnsley.'

'Well, it's a right odd name. I'm Obadiah Spark and this is Mazik Spark.'

'Pleased to meet you, Obadiah Spark and Mazik Spark. I'm glad I'm not the only one with a strange name.'

'Nowt wrong wi' "Obadiah". Right gradley, some would say!'

'Pardon?!'

'Don't worry,' said Mazik. 'Gramps is from Yorkshire. You have to make allowances.'

'I thought this was England, 7th October.'

'Aye, t'is. Mi golden weddin' 'versary! Grand! Any road up, what's tha doin' landin' in garden in yon contraption? Where's tha from, lad, York or Barnsley? Speak up!'

The spaceman's irises seemed to spin. He wondered if Obadiah Spark was teasing him or just confused. 'I'm from *Qua*. I was just cruising around to see where Dr James Spark lives. I went to his house but there was no reply. So I thought I'd try his relatives, as you live so close.'

'Oh, tha kens our Jimmy, does tha?'

Yorke frowned.

'Do you know James?' interpreted Mazik, helpfully.

'He recently returned from a space flight to the mineral-rich asteroid *Paulinus 627*,' replied Yorke.

'World famous, round 'ere, is our lad!' said Gramps.

'He's my big brother,' said Mazik proudly – though he felt that twinge of envy inside.

'Is he here?' asked Yorke.

'Nay, lad, 'e's busy, these days. We don't see 'im, much.'

'He pops in, now and then. He'll be here tonight,' explained Mazik.

'Well, just tell him Yorke Barnsley came by.'

In truth, the spaceman hadn't been casually cruising around to see where Jimmy lived. His aim all along had been to find Mazik, without making it obvious. He had secret plans for the energetic young lad. He bobbed his head back inside, pretending to close the hatch, when Gramps said, 'Where's thee off to, now? Can't tha stay f'dinner?'

'Gramps means "lunch". Are you hungry?'

The spaceman's irises spun again and he muttered, 'Earth food, twenty-first century.' Then he nodded. 'Yes, please, this should be fascinating!' He clambered out wearing a brightly shimmering, silky, booted onesie.

'That's a pretty suit,' said Gramps, exchanging glances with Mazik.

'It's the latest in smart suits. The material is called *fabar*. Erm...for "Fabric from Barnsley"!' he improvised. 'Keeps me at a comfortable temperature, whatever the weather. Hard-wearing and self-cleaning, with full diagnostics and integral biometrics.'

'Bit of a nuisance for spending a penny!' chuckled Gramps.

Yorke's irises spun again. 'Ah, I see what you mean. No, I don't need to worry about such things. I have internal waste processing. I eject a solid capsule full of rich nutrients and essential minerals for recycling.'

'Sounds handy!' replied Gramps, disguising his doubts.

~

Gramps went into the kitchen and started laying the table. 'Tek a seat, lad. Ah'll fix dinner.' Then he shouted into the house, 'Ey up, our lass: dinner! A friend of Jimmy's has arrived from Barnsley.' He winked at Mazik.

'Ah, Grandma. This is Yorke, from Barnsley. He's come to see our Jimmy.'

Grandma was far too polite to remark on Yorke's electric blue complexion. 'Oh, if you're cold, do sit by the radiator. You should have telephoned, first, to see if Jimmy was in. All the way from Barnsley? Do join us for lunch. You must be hungry after your long journey.' Luckily, she didn't notice the spacecraft on the back lawn.

'Thank you, Mrs Spark. I've only come a parsec or two, this morning.' She was distracted and didn't listen properly, but still nodded kindly.

'Well, that's not too far. Help yourself, it's all vegetarian.'

'But you can't travel a parsec in a morning, Yorke,' whispered Mazik, as an aside to the spaceman.

'Not if you're restricted to the speed of light,' answered Yorke, mysteriously.

Mazik frowned. He was sure Yorke couldn't travel faster than light and decided he must be joking. 'Oh, I get it,' he bluffed. 'Would you like to see my football cards after lunch?'

'That would be *very* interesting, I'm sure,' said Yorke, tactfully.

'You can test me. There are no players from Barnsley.'

'But...' It was Yorke's turn to be teased.

'That's very pretty material, Yorke. Did you get it from Marks & Spencer?' asked Grandma.

Yorke's irises went into another mesmeric whirl as he retrieved data from his third-tier memory. 'No...I don't think it's in the shops yet,' he quickly improvised. 'My...er...girlfriend is...er...a fashion designer,' he sounded a little robotic.

'Well, she'll do very well with such beautiful fabric. You must give me her address.'

'Oh, yes...Jimmy has her contact details,' he fibbed uncomfortably. 'I'll ask him to pass them on.' He desperately needed to change the subject, so put some food in his mouth. 'These are olives,' he said robotically. They heard a faint whirring noise. 'I mean, these olives are delicious.' Then he popped in a fig, followed by a piece of mature cheese, a pickled gherkin, an unpeeled tangerine and then some curried coconut; each accompanied by a whirring noise and spinning irises. 'Most interesting combination.' He then put some salt on a spoon and tried that, followed by a spoonful of pepper and the jar of mustard in one swallow. 'Mmm. Fascinating sensation!'

'We don't normally mix food like that, in High Woodley,' said Mazik. 'Fancy some chocolate cake with onion soup dressing and a hot chili curry topping for dessert? I hear it's all the rage in Barnsley!'

Gramps was staring in disbelief, but Mrs Spark was reading the economics page in the *Financial Daily* and didn't notice Yorke drinking the spicy ketchup. Yorke blew out a long stream of steamy vapour. A rainbow crossed his face, there was a

phut

and he put his hand in his pocket and took out a solid capsule. 'Put it on your compost heap, Obadiah: you'll be *delighted* with the results!'

'Ta, muchly! But what is it?' asked Gramps.
'*QuanTum.*'

Gramps pocketed it warily. 'Ah'll clear up in a mo, Grandma,' he said. Then he led Mazik and Yorke back into the garden. 'Must be a right strange place tha's come from, Cap'n Barnsley. Surely tha's not from Bradford?'

'No, sir, but you're welcome to come and visit,' offered the spaceman invitingly. 'We can go there now and I'll have you back before Earth time has moved on.'

'You travel quicker than light?' said Mazik.

'Sort of,' replied Yorke. 'But only in four dimensions.'

'Back in time?' asked Mazik.

'That's not possible.'

'So, you've not come back from a more advanced, future civilisation?'

'More, travelled sideways from a parallel universe. A space-time shift.' Mazik nodded as though he understood it all perfectly. Yorke continued, 'Most of our knowledge came as a result of our recent meeting with Jimmy's space mission.'

'Wow, wait 'til I tell my class!'

~

Bright as the Sparks were, Yorke had been toying with them. His aim all along wasn't to visit Jimmy, but had been to entice Mazik into space, where he could, discreetly, share a little magic.

A small step that would have unimaginable consequences.

~

As they climbed into the spacecraft, Gramps was full of awe and apprehension, but Mazik was fearless. *I'll show that Jammy Jimmy!* he thought. They got in and sat comfortably in the reclining seats. Though the craft's walls looked solid from the outside, they were transparent from the inside, so Gramps and Mazik could see everything around them. Soundlessly, the vehicle lifted off and glided around High Woodley, hovering over the local sports arena, *Revolution!*

'We'll be seen,' said Mazik.

'No, I turned on the visibility mask when I landed so you could see me, but it's off now and nobody can detect us.'

'Magic! What happens if I pull this lever?' said Mazik, pulling the lever.

He looked out and Earth was a shiny, distant, blue disk.

Whoops!

'Give over, lad!' said Gramps angrily. 'We've missed best part!'

'Don't worry we can zoom back down,' said Yorke. 'But it's best not to fiddle with the controls, Mazik.'

'Sorry. I was just curious. What does this do?' Yorke and Gramps swooped on Mazik before he could cause further havoc.

'That one varies the shading of the outer shell. If we're near the sun, we can tint the transparent shell. Or, if we're in the sky over the earth, we can appear the same colour as the sky, whether it's sunny or cloudy. You can play with that one, but you won't see the colours change from inside.'

'I'll just set a course for Earth orbit,' said Yorke.

Mazik was looking round at all the internal controls. 'Look out o'winder, tha daft 'apeth,' urged Gramps. 'Tha'll ne'er get chance, again!'

'Yeah, I know: I'll take some photos. Yorke, you lean in towards Gramps by the window and I'll take a shot with Earth in the background. Smile!'

'Now take one of yourself, Mazik, with an Earth backdrop,' said Yorke, pushing Mazik's index finger aside and pressing the selfie toggle. As Yorke brushed against him, Mazik sensed an electric pulse, surging power through his entire body.

It felt more than reassuring. It was somehow inspiring! Yorke winked at him, knowingly.

Mazik took the selfie. But, when he looked at it, his face was all the colours of Earth! He gasped, astonished, but, before he could speak, Yorke asked, 'Where would you like to go next?'

'Where do you live?' asked Gramps.

'It's a long way off. Probably a couple of gigaparsecs.'

'*How far?*' queried Mazik.

'One gigaparsec is just over three-and-a-quarter billion light-years. So, say six-and-a-half thousand million light-years, travelling at 186,000 miles a second.'

'We'll be late for tea!' said Mazik, 'and my tummy's rumbling, now! Do you have Chococino and a rocky road on this

space cart?' Yorke tapped a few keys and a hatch opened in front of Mazik's seat. 'Wow! Cool!' said Mazik, stuffing his face with cake and gazing out of the window.

'What happens if I press...'

Whoooosh!

Everything went black inside the craft and spirals of light gyrated in the vastness of space. Gramps' shout was distant, warped; his voice distorted:

'Ya daft beggar!'

The craft bucked swayed and spun wildly as their seat belts automatically tightened. Cake and Chococino redecorated the interior.

Finally, the buffeting settled, the spinning stopped and the craft resumed a steady cruise.

'...this button?' finished Mazik.

'I wouldn't have chosen the black-hole route, myself,' said Yorke, mopping up the mess. 'But it is quick. Welcome to *Qua*.'

'What have ah just told thee, lad? Just don't push no more buttons, levers, keys or *thingummyjigs*! If tha knows nowt, do nowt! Tha'll get uz all killed and ah'm not wearing mi funeral suit!'

'Whoops! Soz, Gramps!'

'Ah've got manky rocky road in mi vest, now.'

'Where's *Qua*, Yorke?'

'It doesn't occupy a specific place. It's an entity, but not a physical one.'

'What is it? An invisible cloud?' joked Mazik.

'Pretty much.'

'Never!'

Yorke explained, '*Qua* memorized everything worthwhile that is online on Earth.'

The utter vastness of this achievement seemed to escape Mazik, who had gone silent for a moment. The combination of rocky road and hypersonic travel seemed to be having an urgent effect on his digestion.

'I need a poo!'

Yorke was shocked. He simply ejected perfectly hygienic *QuanTum* capsules and had never encountered the urgency of a small person in great need. 'Hold tight!' he shouted. Then he hit the Home key on the navigation panel. The bucking, swaying and spinning started again, as the vortex of stars circled around them at phenomenal speed. Once the rock 'n' roll had stopped, the craft cruised to a gentle touchdown in Gramps' back garden.

~

Mazik and Gramps climbed out. Yorke stood looking out of the hatchway. 'It's been fun. So long and thanks for all the food!' He was about to close the hatch, but hesitated. 'I'll send a special gift to share with everyone on the big day!' Mazik had no idea what he meant.

The craft swooshed and vanished, leaving them mystified by his parting words.

'Did that actually happen, Gramps?'

''Appen it did, lad,' said Gramps, pointing at a roll of shimmering *fabar* material on the lawn where Yorke's craft had just vanished. He stooped to pick it up.

The fabric sparkled in silky hues of gold. 'Eh up, lad, that'll do nicely for Grandma Lucy's 'versary pressie,' he said gratefully. He had quite forgotten to buy Grandma anything, despite having known for half a century that it was going to be their golden wedding anniversary.

He slipped inside to wrap the gift, craftily avoiding Grandma, who now appeared and asked, 'Where's your Gramps, Mazik? He said he'd clear lunch a moment ago.'

Mazik replied, 'He says he's been to outer space with Yorke, or was it Barnsley?'

Grandma tutted and shook her head in disbelief. Suddenly, Mazik's urgency returned. 'Can't stop to chat, Grandma. Need bad!' and he rushed inside.

~

Gramps came back into the garden just as Mazik reappeared. Gramps put his hand in his pocket and pulled out Yorke's waste capsule of *QuanTum*.

'Ah think ah'll just bury this in compost heap.' They went off to get spades and Mazik helped him dig the compost.

~

The rest of the family arrived in the early evening: Jimmy and Harmony; Mazik's mother, Amy and his big sister, Annie. They all lived nearby. Gramps poured out the champagne and presented Grandma with the fabric. 'This is why Yorke was here,' he fibbed. 'He was delivering it from mill in Barnsley.'

Grandma unwrapped it and was utterly enthralled with the marvellous *fabar* material. The iridescent fabric had the soft smoothness of silk. Everyone fussed over it and asked Gramps how he'd found it. He was vague and just winked at Mazik. Grandma was delighted. She'd be the envy of the High Woodley branch of LEEDS, the Local Economic and Ecological Discussion Society, at their next monthly meeting in the Green Café at *Revolution!*

~

The champagne had gone straight to Harmony's head. She was skilled in the art of dressmaking

and, without thinking, just blurted out, above the hubbub, 'I could make my wedding dress out of this material!'

The room fell into stunned silence.

She put her finger to her lips, looked skywards and blushed deeply.

'Er, whoops!'

Everyone erupted in delighted laughter.

She and Jimmy were bombarded with excited questions about the wedding. Later, when it was a little quieter, Jimmy and Harmony took Mazik aside and asked him who he thought Yorke was. 'Yorke took me and Gramps to a place he called *Qua*. Except it wasn't a place.' Mazik glowed in the satisfaction that now he'd done something Jimmy hadn't.

Jimmy was sure that Yorke was a humanoid manifestation – an avatar of *Qua* – and that the *fabar* material was extra-terrestrial. He dropped an eyebrow at Mazik and said, 'Explain.'

Mazik slapped his forehead, gave Jimmy an exasperated look and decided he'd better explain in plain English to Harmony who he thought far more intelligent than 'Dim Jim'.

'Yorke Barnsley came here in his space cart and took me and Gramps for a ride a long, long way away – two megaparsecs, I think – to something he said was an entity, whatever that is, made of germs or particles or something, called *Qua*. He said he was a friend of Jimmy's. He had a blue face and wore a silky, *fabar* onesie. When he brought us home, he left some of the *fabar* material that Gramps just gave to Grandma Lucy.'

Harmony also immediately realised that Yorke was an avatar from *Qua*. 'Probably best to keep that a secret between us, Mazik,' she whispered, winking confidentially. 'OK?'

'Yeah, a secret between you and me,' whispered Mazik, who was utterly besotted by Harmony.

Mazik knew that Jimmy was very far from dim. He just thought it, sometimes, so that Jimmy fell short of utter perfection. That irritating tweak of envy returned to nip his senses as he realized he'd forgotten to pass on Yorke's message to Jimmy: 'I'll send a special gift to share with everyone on the big day!' At least Mazik now knew what the big day was. *Never mind*, he consoled himself. *It's probably not important.*

~

For Gramps, it was late when he got up the next morning – six-thirty! He was normally up by six to do his weight training, but the family had stayed over, talking until late, about the forthcoming wedding. Gramps put on his shorts and the kettle and then went out, wearing the flat cap he'd slept in, to inspect the compost heap.

He was astounded to find that it had turned into the most luxuriant, nutritious fertiliser he'd ever seen. When everyone but Mazik had gone, they dug it into the vegetable patch, planted the spring vegetable seeds and then spread the compost generously around the soft fruit. With a gentle murmuring hum, all the weeds were sucked into the ground, as, before their eyes, the tips of the swelling seedlings and fruit buds sprouted spontaneously.

Gramps and Mazik were transfixed; deep in thought at the awesome power of *QuanTum*.

Chapter 3

Hot Headers

After school, Mazik strolled to the Green Café at *Revolution!*, where he met his grandparents. Mazik was out of energy, so they quickly ordered food and drinks. Mazik was craving rocky road and Chococino. He hadn't had that since he'd 'redecorated' the inside of Yorke's spacecraft.

As he now ate, Gramps looked with increasing alarm into Mazik's face. Grandma was absorbed in the latest copy of the Ecology Party's weekly bulletin, *Green News*.

'Is anything the matter, Gramps?' asked Mazik, making a quiet whirring noise. He took a gulp of his drink and blew out a stream of steamy vapour.

'Eh, lad, tha eyes have gone just like Captain Barnsley's when he was thinkin' of summat, or eatin', tha knows. Them irises are sort of whizzin' whirligigs. It's weirdly hypnotic. Does tha feel sick or owt?'

'No, Gramps. I feel quite normal, really. In fact...' Mazik stopped dead, mid-sentence. He screwed his eyes up and his hair stood on end. Then he

squeezed and pushed

with a

squelch and a squinch

'Oh, cripes!' There was a gentle pop and Mazik lifted his T-shirt. In his belly button was a *QuanTum* capsule! Exactly as Yorke Barnsley had given to Gramps to fertilize the compost heap.

'Oh, bother! I've laid an egg!' said Mazik, his voice an octave deeper than normal. He gently pulled the cylinder-shaped capsule out. 'It's a crapsule!' He held it up. 'Should I put it on the vegetable patch, Gramps?'

Gramps was too stunned to speak for a moment. 'Ah don't rightly know, lad. P'raps, but ah've already put loads of *QuanTum* on veg patch. If thee puts even more on, tha'll have lettuce trees and carrot bushes – goosegogs the size of footballs and blackberries like cannonballs!'

Mazik hadn't been listening.

Instead, he'd been inspecting the capsule, looking at the tiny glittering crystals in its surface. It spoke to his inner spark.

He could resist its lure if he really tried, but, instinctively, he knew that great strength could come of the momentous act he was about to perform. He murmured, 'I wonder what'll happen if I...'

No!

screamed Gramps, but it was too late. 'Tha daft chump! Ya shouldn'a done that! Who knows what's in it?!'

Mazik had purposely swallowed the *QuanTum* whole! He'd not smelled it or licked it but, quite deliberately, knowingly, just downed the entire capsule in one, great gulp! Nothing happened for several seconds. Then, his hair turned emerald green and spiked out like a hedgehog. His eyes were as round as saucers and his irises started spinning, but this time at high speed. His arms pulsed with swirling patterns in countless shades and tiny, multi-coloured spotlights shone from every freckle.

He put his tongue out.

Rainbow colours splashed and pulsated on it.

A rumble started deep down in his bowels and rose explosively through his stomach, up into his chest. The volcanic belch he let out rattled the café windows. Passers-by looked in, to see if a bomb had gone off.

Grandma put her paper down and looked quizzically at Mazik as he stood up. He'd grown ten centimetres. There was a gap between the bottom of his T-shirt and his waistband, which wasn't there before.

Gramps' eyes bulged. His jaw hung loose. He tried to speak, but nothing came out. Grandma raised her paper and carried on reading.

Mazik sat down heavily and said, 'Well that beats rocky road!' His hair had settled down and faded. His tongue and arms were no longer quivering in dazzling shades and designs. His eyes were back to steady, jet black. He sat there grinning idiotically.

'What'll tha mother say?' asked Gramps. 'She'll say we're too careless to look after thee! Ah'll be in right trouble, now!'

'I'll just say I've had a sudden growth spurt.'

'Growth spurt! Tha's eaten tha own compost, tha brainless wee twit! Does tha feel nowt?'

'I feel normal again, now, really. Just a bit hungry. Can I have another rocky road?'

'Grandma, can he have another rocky road?'

'It'll spoil tea!'

'Have an apple, lad. But no more tricks! Fancy eatin' *QuanTum*! Tha gets dafter every day! Look, tha trouser bottoms are three inches above tha shoe tops. We'd best visit charity clothes shop, on way home.'

'Gramps, I think you should try one!'

'Tha mus' be jokin', son. Tha won't catch me eatin' manure.'

'And rub some on your bald patch too!'

'Listen up, tha senseless wee halfwit, ah'm neither eatin' stuff, nor rubbin' it on deficient parts of mi anatomy. Ah'm very happy with bald pate and diminutive stature, thankin' thee. Five foot three suits me very nicely, ta, muchly.'

~

Over the next week, when he went to his grandparents' after school, Mazik took to having his snack privately in the summerhouse. He claimed that he was bird watching for a nature project. After each snack, he reacted as he had done in the Green Café, but now he collected the daily capsules in one of his empty football card tins, marked *Hot Headers*.

When he felt he had enough for his artful plan, he added a little water and the *QuanTum* dissolved into a paste. He sealed the tin tightly, put an elastic band around it and slipped a

small, broad paintbrush under the band. He put the tin in his school bag.

This was very pleasing on several counts. Not only was it a most enjoyable sensation, producing the capsules, but it satisfied his passion to collect and also, to do something secretly, with a specific purpose in mind.

~

While Gramps was snoozing in his armchair in the lounge and Grandma was catching up with the weekly *Green News* in the kitchen, Mazik crept into the lounge. He took out his *Hot Headers* tin and slipped behind Gramps' armchair.

Gramps was snoring rhythmically and hardly moved as Mazik carefully removed Gramps' best flat cap and with great deliberation, painted his shiny bald head with the *Hot Headers* paste.

Mazik replaced the tin in his bag and sat cross-legged in front of Gramps, eagerly awaiting the outcome of the experiment. Gradually, a golden glow spread from the top of Gramps' head, down his face and neck, until his hands were also glowing gold. Bands of yellow surged down his face, gradually darkening, until the top of his head was black.

He gave a deep snort, shuffled around in his sleep, muttered, 'Small and bald, but devastatingly handsome and smart,' then fell into a deeper slumber. Now, his dome steadily returned to its normal tone. Mazik stood up and looked at him closely. *Wouldn't it be great if everyone could change colour like that!* he thought. Suddenly, he saw little spikes of black hair growing out of the shiny, bald scalp.

In his sleep, Gramps raised his hand and scrubbed the top of his head with his palm, as though it itched. Mazik rushed off to get the hand mirror and, by the time he'd returned, Gramps' scalp was covered with fine shoots of hair and his head was gently steaming. *Hot Headers!* thought Mazik, as Gramps was waking up.

'Er, Gramps?'

'Yes, son. Ah just had forty winks!'

'Er, Gramps? How do you feel?' said Mazik, hesitantly.

'Ah feel fine, thankin' thee!'

He scratched his scalp.

'What! What's goin' on? What has tha bin up to, young tyke?' yelled Gramps, rising out of the armchair.

Mazik held up the mirror and Gramps collapsed back into the chair. Mazik braced himself for an explosion of anger.

'Blinkin' ummers! Has tha stuck rug on mi 'ead?'

'No, Gramps, I've just been sitting here waiting for you to wake up.'

Gramps grabbed the mirror and looked closely. 'Ee, mi 'airs growin' like rhubarb. I can 'ear it!'

'Blinkin' marvellous!' laughed Gramps, to Mazik's huge relief. 'Ah've not had hair forty years' since! Ah mus' show our lass!'

He got up and called, 'Lucy, look as uz bonce! Jus' come 'n' look! It's a miracle! Wonderful! Ah've got an 'ead full of 'air!' He danced a little jig in the hallway. 'Aye and its original colour too: black!'

Stop growing, stop growing! Mazik was saying to himself in alarm. *I've put too much on: I didn't know how much to use. It's much stronger than I thought.*

Gramps' hair was creeping over his collar and he was transfixed by the sight in the mirror.

By the time Grandma came to see, Gramps' hair was shoulder length. 'Oo, ah look like a lass! Best rush down to barber's. Not been to barber's these fifty year. Not since uz weddin'! Hee, hee, look at this, our lass!'

'Obadiah Spark, what have you been up to, now? You stupid old fool!'

'Nowt, lass. Ah were asleep. Ask our Mazik.'

At that point, Grandma and Gramps looked meaningfully at each other, then searchingly at Mazik, 'Are you sure you've not done anything... naughty?' asked Grandma. 'Now's the best time to confess!' Mazik looked desperate.

'Ee, don't worry, lad: it's a marvel. Ah'm delighted!' and Gramps' face sparkled like an excited child.

'Mmm, well maybe, er...maybe...' Mazik scrambled to think of something convincing. '...you've rubbed your head with the gardening gloves you used for spreading the *QuanTum* compost – you were wearing them in goal, earlier!'

'Aye, tha's right, lad. It's manure what's done it! Good job it were only mi 'ead ah scratched!' Gramps thought this hilarious and belly-laughed uncontrollably for ages.

By the time he'd recovered, the hair had stopped sprouting. He had a lush, black mane and looked forty years younger. He skipped around the house, looking in every mirror, saying, 'Wonderful! Extraordinary!' He kept tugging his new locks, just to check they were real.

Grandma sat in her chair, wept a little, then laughed, shook her head and muttered 'Silly little man!'

Then, she continued reading *Green News*.

When Amy came to collect Mazik, she marvelled at Gramps' transformation.

While Gramps gave Mazik his usual parting grapple, he whispered, 'Ah've peeped in tha school bag, young Mazik. Gardenin' gloves, my backside! Ah've got tha *Hot Headers* tin of compost paste in uz pocket. Safest place for it! Ah can't imagine what tha'd get up to wi' such powerful stuff! Ah'll see thee next week and we'll discuss it then, when tha's more sense in tha daft bonce!'

Chapter 4

All Change!

The following week, when Mazik came around, Gramps confronted him. 'Now, lad, tha'd best explain what tha's been up to wi' yon *QuanTum*.'

'I've been making it myself, then mixing it into a paste in the tin.'

'And why would that be, son?' frowned Gramps.

'At first, it was just somewhere to keep it, in case I ever needed some.'

'And then?'

'The thing is, it seems to get stronger the longer it's left.'

'In that case, it's a good job tha painted mi bonce when tha did and no later, otherwise ah'd have sprouted hair like a horse's mane. Best be careful, young man, or tha'll be arrested for gross expansion! Any road up, does tha know what ah've got in uz pocket, young Mazik?'

'Something snotty?'

'Nay, lad, summat proper! Nowt disgustin'.'

Mazik groaned. 'Is it a boring, old coin again, Gramps?'

'Aye, tha's right. Good guess, lad,' said Gramps proudly. 'Here, have a gander at this.' Gramps slipped a piece of red velvet out of his pocket and carefully unwrapped a tiny, shiny gold coin. 'Does tha know what it be?'

'I'm sure you're about to tell me in excruciating detail, Gramps,' said Mazik, stifling a yawn and slumping in his chair.

'It be *the* oldest English coin. *The* oldest!' he emphasised. 'Issued in London by Archbishop Smellytoes around 604AD. Unique! Unique!' cried Gramps, bouncing excitedly.

'Wow!' said Mazik, suddenly sitting up and paying attention. 'The first English coin ever, ever, ever?'

'Aye, proper English, not Roman, mind. And ah found it mi'sen, in one of them muddy holes ah dug!'

'Do you want to see *my* new thing, Gramps?' asked Mazik, changing the subject.

'Is this like last *thing* – swallowin' *QuanTum* crapsule?'

Mazik put the gold coin down on the velvet. 'Watch this, Gramps.' He stared hard at the coin and Gramps watched.

Mazik shut his eyes, muttered *Barnsley* to himself and suddenly the portrait on the coin turned into Gramps and winked at them.

'What the blinkin' ummers!' panicked Gramps, leaping to his feet and grasping handfuls of hair. The original portrait reappeared.

'Phew!' sighed Gramps, perspiring with relief. He quickly wrapped the coin in the velvet and stuffed it safely back in his pocket. 'Ah thought mi heart had stopped beatin'! Give over, will thee! Doin' them right daft stunts wi' mi best coin. It's not good for elderly, havin' a shock!'

'Sorry. Are you okay?'

'Aye,' said Gramps mopping his brow. 'Any road up, what's yon new trick about?'

'I can change things around!'

'How long has tha known? No, don't tell uz, since uz trip to end of universe in Yorke Barnsley's spacecraft! Aye, of course, he could mek craft transparent! Is that it, cheeky monkey?'

'I guess so, Gramps. Maybe that, plus swallowing the *QuanTum* crapsule. It started after we'd got back from space. I thought I was going mad, at first. I'd go to pick up my eraser and it was gone. Erased itself. Then it would reappear as something else. It was random, until I learnt a trick to control it: I just have to concentrate, then trigger it by saying *Barnsley*, in my head!'

'Magic, Mazik, pure magic! Has tha tried it on owt big, yet? Not on a 'uman bein', I hope?'

'No! I've not tried it on a person!'

'Good, best not to. What's biggest thing tha's disappeared?'

'Annie's old doll. I didn't think she'd care, at her age, but she went berserk looking for it, before I reappeared it!'

'That's a right bad thing to do! If tha's mean with power, tha'll lose it! And worse.'

'I know. I couldn't disappear anything, the rest of that day.'

~

A couple of days later, Gramps' mobile phone rang. He picked it up, warily. 'Hi, Gramps!' said Mazik. 'I've got tomorrow off. It's a training day. We could play Gutterball.'

'Ah were goin' to plant winter veg.'

'Can't you do that later?' pleaded Mazik.

'S'pose so.' Gramps thought for a moment. 'Does tha want to go to Science Museum?'

'Yeah! And the Natural History Museum.'

'Best come for sleepover. Then we can set out bright and early! Ah'll get tickets.'

'Great! I'll get Mum to bring me over after tea.'

'Aye, after supper. Ah'll tell Grandma Lucy to expect *trouble*! None of tha tricks while we're in town, mind!'

'Of course not, Gramps. See you later!'

The following morning, they took the tube from High Woodley station and changed onto the Piccadilly Line, westbound. It was crowded, but someone kindly made room for Gramps and he sat down. Mazik squeezed in beside him and Gramps, promptly nodded off.

They'd just passed Hyde Park Corner and Mazik was watching a woman opposite doing a crossword with her friend, when a tall, bald, bearded man in a brown suit stepped in front of him. He was carrying a briefcase with his name on it, "Harry Ramsbottom". His dog – a huge golden retriever – stood obediently beside him. Its collar was embroidered *Goldie Wagtail*.

The carriage swayed and it was very warm. Mazik leaned back against Gramps and closed his eyes. He heard the crossword woman say, '16 across: a town in South Yorkshire, eight letters, starting with 'B'?'

Her colleague answered 'Barnsley'. Mazik's eyes sprang open and he was aghast to see that the man now had the dog's hairy head and long ears and the retriever was bald and bearded.

The eyes of the woman opposite bulged.

Mazik waved, stuck his finger up his nose and wiggled it around energetically, as if he'd caught something big. The woman looked horrified, immediately raised her newspaper and remained stubbornly hidden behind it for the rest of her journey.

A smart young woman, with shoulder-length, golden-brown hair and an elegant purple suit, now stood in front of Mazik. He shut his eyes tightly. The man sitting next to him was talking to his wife. 'They're moving up to somewhere in South Yorkshire. Swapping their little London terraced house for a mansion. I think he said... Barnsley.'

Mazik's eyes shot open, expecting the worst.

The smart, young woman now had the dog's hairy head and long ears and the man had shoulder-length golden-brown hair.

Mazik squeezed his eyes firmly shut again and shouted as loud as he could inside his head: *Barnsley!*

He opened his eyes.

The woman in the purple suit was now bald.

Goldie Wagtail had long golden-brown hair and Harry Ramsbottom sported the golden retriever's long tail.

He should be called 'Hairy Dogsbottom', thought Mazik before starting to panic.

Suddenly, he was flushed with guilt. He knew that when he shouted *Barnsley!* in his head, a part of his mind had positively wanted something outrageous to happen.

But now he thought the magic words in earnest: *Barnsley! Barnsley! Barnsley! Barnsley!*

He struggled to control his rising dread but forced his eyes open.

He grimaced.

Harry now had dog's legs; Goldie wore brown trousers and the once-elegant young woman had a bearded forehead.

Mazik screwed his eyes up and yelled in his head, *Yorke Barnsley! If you don't sort me out, immediately, I'll die of embarrassment!*

He opened his eyes.

Harry Ramsbottom and Goldie were, thankfully, restored to their proper state. Mazik gave a huge sigh of relief.

But he couldn't see the young woman's head, as she'd turned to gather her bags and step off the train.

As she strode onto the platform, he caught sight of her and nearly screamed with horror.

'Gramps!' He dug his elbow into Gramps' stomach. 'Wake up!'

'What? Where are we? Ah dozed off! Have we missed uz station?'

The train was gathering speed out of Knightsbridge station. 'We need to get off and chase that lady.' Mazik pointed out of the window.

Gramps nearly had a fit: The woman had a huge tail hanging out of the back of her head.

'Tha can't just chase young ladies. Chase her where?'

'I took a photo with my mobile, look.'

She wore a lapel badge, reading:

Harold's Cosmetics

'Right,' said Gramps. 'Best get off at next stop – South Kensington – and double back to Harold's!'

Gramps patted Goldie's head as they stood anxiously waiting for the train to stop. Then, they rushed off, ran to the eastbound platform and hopped onto a waiting train, just before the doors shut.

'Didn't I say *do nowt daft*!?'

'Sorry, Gramps! It wasn't my fault. The woman opposite had 'Barnsley' as a crossword answer and the man next to me had friends moving there. Everything just spun horribly out of control! Yorke did it on purpose.' A big tear splodged down his face onto the floor.

Gramps hugged him. 'Don't tek badly, son. We'll sort it out! C'mon, cheer up. Look what ah've got in mi pocket.'

'Is it Archbishop Smellytoes' shilling?' sniffed Mazik.

'Nay, lad, it's big bar a Gramps' secret chocolate! That'll cheer thee up! Tha can disappear that into tha stomach!'

'Thanks, Gramps!'

They soon arrived back at Knightsbridge and rushed out of the station.

'Ah can't keep up wi' thee, young 'un. It's mi feet tha knows!'

'Look, there's a sign for Harold's. Come on, quickly! Hurry up, Gramps!' They dodged through the traffic and entered the swanky store right opposite the Cosmetics Hall.

They scanned the counters, before Mazik shouted, 'Look there she is!' She was serving at one of the counters, under a banner:

COSMETICS FOR THE CHIC
WITH MORE DOLLARS THAN SCENTS

'By 'eck, that were lucky! What to do now, our Mazik?'

'You go and buy something from her. Keep her talking and I'll see if I can magic away the tail.'

Gramps shuffled up to the counter, already red in the face and perspiring from their dash. He'd never chatted to an attractive, young woman at a cosmetics counter, let alone one adorned with a beautiful, long, retriever tail.

'Oh, hello luv, ah mean miss. Um…ah mean… has tha owt smelly? Ah mean, y'know, fragrant, for uz missus like?' His face was now bright red.

'Of course, sir, what does she like? Would you like to try this?' She sprayed something on the inside of her wrist and offered it to him. As he sniffed, he turned the same purple as her suit.

'Oo, aye,'eck. What is it?' His heart was pounding. He couldn't stop himself blurting out, 'How much does it cost, luv? Ah mean, miss?'

'It's only a hundred pounds a bottle,' she answered, casually.

Gramps turned the tiny bottle around in his hand. His mouth opened, but no sound came out.

'If it's not to your liking, perhaps your wife would prefer something from the lingerie department?'

Gramps complexion had now deepened to pickled beetroot. He could feel beads of sweat running off his scalp and down his back. His new mane of thick hair wasn't helping. He wished the ground would just open up and swallow him whole.

By this time, Mazik was hiding on the far side of the counter.

He could see the woman's tail quite clearly. He stared for a moment, squeezed his eyes shut and repeated the magic spell in his head.

He opened his eyes.

Out of the sides of her head grew a pair of enormous, hairy, floppy retriever ears. The long tail wagged happily.

Mazik shut his eyes. *Yorke Barnsley, if you think this is funny, I'll come into outer space and shove one of your capsules where it really hurts.*

Once again, he shouted *Barnsley!* in his head.

He slowly opened his eyes. The woman's lush, golden-brown hair swept thickly in long waves to her slender shoulders.

Phew! thought Mazik. *I'm never using that power again! How could she have walked across town without someone noticing? Incredible! Perhaps it's the latest fashion!* He sidled round and stood next to Gramps who was now holding something in a pretty pink packet. Beads of sweat ran down his forehead in little rivulets.

Mazik gave a thumbs-up and grinned. 'OK, Gramps!' Then he did a startled double take. The shop assistant must have changed her lapel badge on arrival. It now read:

As they drifted away from the counter, Mazik laughed. 'Goldie Wagtail! That was the dog's name, too!'

Gramps chuckled for a moment but then said anxiously, 'Ah've just spent a small fortune on a tiny bottle of summat called 'Channel Five'! Ah've no clue what it is. Missus'll kill uz!'

'Gramps, I think it's Chanel No. 5. The perfume. Mum loves it! Grandma will be delighted if you give it her for her next birthday.'

'She'll kill uz!' he repeated. 'Any road up, tha daft 'apeth wi' tha silly tricks, just give over!'

'That was nothing, Obadiah the Elderly: you slept through all the best brain bombs!'

~

That night, Mazik lay in bed, looking back in amusement at the events of the day. He couldn't help feeling worried that the strange new talents he'd acquired, undoubtedly from meeting Yorke Barnsley, were out of control. Fortunately it wasn't entirely random, but yet nowhere near being under his total command. He needed to work hard to be in charge of his powers.

But surely these new talents weren't just from meeting Yorke? After all, Gramps had been on the space flight with him and he was still normal – well – normal for Gramps. No, there was more to it than that. Perhaps it was due to eating the *QuanTum* and then producing a capsule himself? One way or another, it all came from *Qua*.

With the lingering thought of the electric surge that Mazik now called *Yorke's spark*, he sank into a deep sleep.

Chapter 5

Sparks Fly

The next morning, Mazik awoke and went to visit his grandparents. Mazik persuaded Gramps to play table football table, in the garage. Just as they were about to start, Mazik suddenly left the ground and floated up to the garage ceiling.

'Whatever next! Tha can't do that in middle of game, lad!' shouted Gramps.

'I didn't do it on purpose!'

'Come down, right now!'

'You'll have to pull me down, Gramps.'

Gramps hauled an old, wooden ladder out of the rafters. 'Ah can't be climbin' ladders at my age, son!'

'And I can't be left floating up on the ceiling at my age, Gramps!'

Muttering under his breath, Gramps climbed up, grabbed Mazik by the ankle and slowly pulled him down, hand-over-hand. When their heads were level, Gramps gave Mazik a baffled frown and a firm pat on the head, which set him drifting back down to the ground.

'Hang on to this ladder while I fetch down mi hobnail boots.' Gramps shuffled the ladder and brought down an old cardboard box. 'I hope mice haven't nested in 'em.'

Luckily, the boots were clean and dry. 'That'll keep tha feet on ground, lad.'

Mazik put them on, though they were far too big.

'Thanks, Gramps! I was winning 5–0 before I floated away.' He dragged his feet in Gramps' heavy boots across to the other side of the football table and rolled in another ball. It bounced straight off a midfielder and directly into the goal. '6–0! C'mon, Gramps, I'm trouncing you!'

'Ah weren't ready. Ah'm still up ladder! Anyway, what's tha doin' floatin' t'ceiling?'

'Oh, it's another *thing*, Gramps.'

'Another *thing*! What does tha mean a *thing*? What sort of *thing*?'

'A flying *thing*. I usually grab hold of something when I feel it coming on, but I thought I'd show you what happens.'

'How long has this bin goin' on?'

'Since we flew with Yorke.'

''Appen it's from bein' weightless in space.'

'Perhaps.'

'Ah feel a little light-headed, mi'sen. Does anyone else know about it?'

'Just Doctor Obadiah Spark.'

'Just me?'

'Yes, Gramps. I've not told anyone else.'

'And it hasn't happened at school? Ah mean, suddenly floatin' off in middle of borin' lesson?'

'I usually manage to hold onto my desk until the feeling has passed. Although, I nearly took the desk with me in art class! The girl next to me thought I'd gone mad. But that's not unusual! At footie, I scored a spectacular goal from an overhead kick!'

'Let's try long jump in garden, Mazik.'

Gramps measured out a run-up to his sandy vegetable patch. He then pegged out ten markers, each a metre apart. 'Have a bash, lad: see how far tha can jump.'

'Gramps, I've got your hobnail boots on. I can hardly lift my feet!'

'Well, put tha trainers back on, dafty! Hurry up, lad.'

Mazik changed his shoes, then took a run-up and launched into the makeshift pit.

'Four metres!' shouted Gramps.

'Is that good, Gramps?'

'Not bad. Run up to tek-off mark as fast as tha can, then push upwards wi' big leap.'

Mazik tried again, running as fast he could.

'Better! Four-and-a-half metres. Give it one more try! When tha hits tek-off point, shout *Barnsley!*'

'Right, Gramps.'

Mazik went to the end of the runway, took three deep breaths and ran as fast as he could to the take-off. As he leapt into the air, he yelled 'Barnsley!' He flew straight over the vegetable patch, bounced on the trampoline, straight over the hedge, onto the neighbour's trampoline, over *their* hedge and landed in the garden pond, two houses down. A pair of ducks squawked angrily.

Gramps rushed round to find Mazik dripping by the pond side. 'Is tha alright, our Mazik? Nowt broke?'

'I might have broken some frogs, Gramps.'

'Ee, tha's lucky! But tha'll have to master flyin'. Best get thee into dry clouts afore Grandma notices! Tha's broke world record for high jump 'n' long jump, young Spark! Could tha control flight?'

'I felt the weightlessness coming on in the run-up. I aimed for the trampoline, but I had no idea what was over the hedge, so that was totally random! But I did try to land in the pond, as I thought I was less likely to hurt myself. I just missed the rockery!'

'So, tha couldna come down from garage ceiling but tha managed to land in yonder pond?'

'I didn't *try* to come down from the garage ceiling: I was curious to see what you had in the rafters!'

'And did tha see owt worthy?'

'Mainly your hundred-year-old rubbish, Gramps!'

'We'll have to keep thee grounded.'

'Grounded! I'm grounded for flying?' moaned Mazik.

'No, lad. I just meant we'll have to try and keep tha feet on ground! Tha can't go to school in huge hobnail boots!'

Mazik changed into dry clothes and they went back into the garage, closing the door behind them.

'Right now, Yuri Gagarin, let's see what tha can do?'

'Who's Yogi Gaga Grin, Gramps?'

'Yuri Gagarin were first spaceman. Russian cosmonaut. Orbited Earth in April 1961. I remember it like it were yesterday.'

'I can't just fly anytime I want. I don't know when it's going to happen.'

'Well, let's just carry on playin' table footie, an' if tha feels a little flighty, just say!'

'I was winning 6–0!'

'Ah were up ladder for last goal!'

'Okay, 5–0. Here we go!'

Mazik dropped the new ball in and it ricocheted randomly around for a while, before Gramps deftly sidestepped Mazik's defenders and slammed in his first goal, '5–1! Here come Obadiah's Owls, hold onto to thy hat, young 'un!'

'Gramps! Gramps! It's happening! Look!'

Mazik was fifteen centimetres above the ground and rising.

'Right, lad. Now tell thysen to keep still. Just hover!'

'Okay!' For a moment, Mazik drifted. He went down a little, bounced off the floor and started rising again.

'Hold steady, lad!'

'I'm trying!' He stopped rising, descended a little, rose a bit, then crashed to the ground.

'Good lad! Tha's gettin' hang of it, now.'

'Can I put your hobnail boots back on, Gramps? I may have better control, then.'

'Aye, lad, tha may be more stable in boots.' Mazik put the boots back on and tied the laces.

'Right, lad. Now, stand still and think of Barnsley.' Nothing happened. 'Is tha thinkin' hard, son?'

Mazik shut his eyes tight, wrinkled his brow and thought as hard as he could about Captain Yorke Barnsley. Suddenly, he was floating a few centimetres above the ground. He opened his eyes. 'Gramps, it worked!'

'Aye, lad, don't talk, just focus on what tha's doin'. Float up so tha feet are level with mi hand.' He held his hand about a metre above the ground. Mazik wobbled upwards and then stopped when his feet were level with Gramps' hand. Gramps held his hand palm up. 'Try 'n' land on hand, lad.' Mazik coasted slowly towards Gramps, then rose a little and came down on Gramps' palm.

'Ee, tha's magic, Mazik, blinkin' magic!' laughed Gramps. Mazik lost concentration and floated up to the rafters.

'Ouch! I banged my head on some old rubbish from the First World War. Don't you ever throw anything out, Gramps?'

'It'll be worth a bob or two, one day. Any road, that's tha inheritance, lad! Now, stop talking and concentrate. Think about floating down t'ground, right?'

'Yes, Gramps!'

'Don't talk, jus' think! Think hard, lad.'

Mazik glided down and landed rather more heavily than he'd intended, as the garage door had started to open.

'7–2!' improvised Mazik, spinning the forward line.

'I sez no spinnin', or else ah'll tek penalty!'

'Are you two still playing table football?'

'First to ten, Grandma!' said Mazik.

'Well, come in when you've finished. It's time for lunch.'

'8–2!' replied Mazik, sinking a clearance direct from his goalie. 'We won't be long now, Grandma!'

The door closed and Mazik shut his eyes tightly. He again thought *Barnsley* and, a moment later, he was airborne. This time he glided to the rafters, back down, touched one wall, then the far wall and finished with an aerial somersault, before landing smoothly.

'That's it, lad, well done! Tha's mastered th'art of 'uman flight! But best keep this twixt thee and me. No need for nosey folk to know, right?'

'I'll have to practise more, so I don't do it accidentally. Like, flying across the goalmouth to make an impossible save! Or floating up to the top shelf in the kitchen, to steal chocolate from Annie's secret stash!'

'We'd best go and get our lunch. Then I'll cycle home with thee. Seein' as tha wakes up at 5:58 every mornin', tha can practice in tha room while t'others is still abed.'

'And when I come here.'

'Aye, lad, but best keep it to thysen!'

~

Mazik took Gramps' advice and improved his flying skills secretly while everyone else was still fast asleep. After a few days, he was confident that he'd controlled the take-off, flight and landing enough to venture a little further. He certainly didn't want anybody, especially his classmates, to know he had weird powers.

He woke rather earlier than his customary 5:58.

He drew the curtains and looked out. It was still dark.

He eased the window open silently, climbed onto the sill and slipped onto the flat roof of the bay window below.

He shut his eyes tightly, thought *Barnsley* and a second later was airborne.

It was thrilling, but he was flying blind, in the dark. The beams of the streetlights were directed downwards, so everything above was in deep shade.

Suddenly, he felt the taut pull of telephone lines across his chest!

Mazik gasped. He was moving too quickly to stop himself being catapulted backwards into the set of telephone lines opposite, which then stretched across his back and propelled him forward again, head-first into the neighbour's tree.

The leaves cushioned the impact and he bounced back to the ground rather heavily. As he fell, he crossed the beam of a security light and was spotlighted on the ground. Mazik froze in horror! What was more, the telephone wires had come down and triggered the neighbours' security alarms. He squeezed his eyes shut and focussed as hard as he could. As soon as he was airborne, he flew straight through his open bedroom window and crash-landed on his bed. He pulled the duvet over his head and snuggled into his pillow for safety.

Very soon, he could hear a commotion. His mother, Amy and big sister, Annie, had rushed outside to see what was going on. All the neighbours had come out in their pyjamas and dressing gowns – all except for Number 16, who was wearing his birthday suit. Mrs 16 was chasing after him with a blanket. Mazik popped his head out from under the duvet, climbed out and peered through the window. He overheard Amy saying, 'The lines are down. That must have triggered the alarms. I can't imagine what caused that; a drone, maybe?'

By now the neighbours had silenced their alarms but the man whose spotlight Mazik had triggered was saying, 'I'll check the security camera and see if anything's been recorded.' Mazik was horrified.

Of course, at breakfast, the mysterious incident was the hot topic. Mazik remained unusually quiet as Annie and Amy discussed what could have caused the disturbance.

'Are you feeling alright, Mazik?' asked Amy.

Annie smiled. 'Don't worry, Mazik, it's probably nothing. Maybe the milkman or a fox triggered the spotlight.'

By the time they'd finished eating, their neighbour had sent Amy a clip of his security camera video.

Mazik was trembling with fright. He'd been discovered on his first flight. How stupid he'd been!

But all that the footage showed was a blurred image of a foot, quickly passing through the beam. It didn't look like it was on the ground.

The neighbour had added a comment. 'Beware the fleet-footed phantom of High Woodley!'

'Phew!' though Mazik, breathing a sigh of relief. He was going to have to be much more careful, in future.

~

The next time he went to his grandparents' after school, Mazik suggested to Gramps that they cycle around the area, for practice. When they set off, he told Gramps what had happened.

'Tha were askin' f'trouble, jumpin' outta bedroom winder afore dawn. Is tha bonkers or summat?'

'Probably. It's your fault, Gramps!'

'Ey up! How d'ya work that out, son?'

'I've inherited your bonkers gene!'

''Appen. But *ah've* never bin catapulted into tree by telephone wires! You'd be better off wearin' mi old hobnail boots to keep thee on ground.'

'Of course! I'll tell Mum I'm to sleep in Gramps' hobnail boots, to stop me floating to the ceiling!'

'Just concentrate on tha cyclin', young man!'

'I'm memorising all the obstacles in the area. All the security lights and cameras triggered by motion. All the lampposts, telegraph posts and telephone lines. All the trees.'

'It'd be simpler not to fly. I tell thee, tha's asking f'trouble!'

'It's too much fun to stop, Gramps! It's even better than football cards!'

~

Next morning, Mazik again woke early; climbed out of his window onto the flat roof below; screwed his eyes up; whispered 'Barnsley'; and slowly took off, vertically. He climbed to just above tree-top height, circled the immediate neighbourhood in the moonlight and glided back into his room.

The following week, he and Gramps again cycled around the neighbourhood after school. This time, Mazik noted all the obstacles between his house and Gramps'. Last thing that night, Mazik dusted off the old toybox, dug out his love-worn, yet abandoned, Biggles Bear – the one with flying goggles and a pilot's leather jacket – and, in his best writing, made a label to tie around Biggles' neck.

Early the next morning, he slipped out of the window. Cautiously, he flew the route to his grandparents' house and carefully landed on the summerhouse roof, leaving Biggles on the apex.

He flew off and pinged a message from his mobile to Gramps. 'Biggles on shed roof!' A moment later, Gramps phoned back. 'Shed? Shed? How dare thee!? That's uz best summer'ouse, ah'll have thee know, young rascal. Any road, has tha got 'uman flyin' licence?'

'Gramps, have you reset your predictive text to Yorkshire dialect?'

'Ah'm up ladder, gettin' young Biggles down. What's this? *Mazik's Air Service. Local deliveries, twopence*! Well, tha's better not let tha Grandma Lucy catch thee flyin' around. She's bound t'clip tha wings, permanent, for certain!' Then Gramps added, 'Reminds me of our Jimmy's skateboard delivery service, when he were your age!'

Mazik felt that twinge of envy, yet again. *Trust Jimmy to always do it first,* he thought and said, hastily, 'Must dash. Bye, Gramps!'

The following week, Mazik and Gramps cycled the route from Mazik's house to Jimmy's, which was also quite close by. Again, Mazik looked out for all the obstacles on the route.

'One day, tha'll do summat right daft and get in trouble. I keep tellin' thee!'

'It's okay, Gramps, I won't get caught.'

'What if tha hits summat, or tha powers disappear mid-flight, all of a sudden?'

'It won't happen, Gramps. Stop worrying. I'm big, now!'

'Ecky thump, lad, tha knows nowt!'

Chapter 6

The Catwalk

Since the publication of *Jammy Jimmy*, James had been receiving invitations to appear at all sorts of venues. He'd accepted some. But, mostly, he'd sent his apologies. He'd just flicked a particularly garish invitation into the waste bin, when Harmony came to help sort the post.

'You can't throw that away!' she gasped.

'Why, what is it?' he asked.

'Only *the* most sought-after invitation in the entire social calendar!' said Harmony, lifting the gilt-edged card out of the bin. 'It's the Annual Ritz Smarmycreep Event!'

'I've never heard of it.'

'That's 'cos you've got your head in the clouds, Dr Spark. Look, we're all invited!'

'But, what is it? Are those initials deliberate?'

'Of course! It's a crazy, absurd, fashion show, but it is incredibly influential. It's *the* trendsetter!'

'I'm not going to a fashion show! All those silly, stick-thin models prancing about.'

'You'll love it. It's hilarious! Bizarre! You won't believe the insane ideas that Spiky Smarmycreep has!'

~

Of course, Harmony had got her way. The invitation was accepted and, when the day of the event arrived, the whole family headed into London to see the show. Harmony had fashioned her own dress specially for the event, from Grandma Lucy's roll of *fabar* material.

She, Annie, Amy and Lucy chattered excitedly as they waited for the Smarmycreep show to start. Jimmy and Mazik sat sullenly behind them, one on either side of Gramps, who grumpily muttered his discomfort and disapproval, until Grandma turned around and gave him a *look*.

~

Spiky Smarmycreep – the top fashion designer – had a global following. People would wear anything that had his label on it. If he'd put his name on thrown-away newspaper wrapping from the local chippy, coated in stale grease and mushy peas, some brainless follower would have worn it.

She would probably wear it balanced on her head, with nothing else on but the Smarmycreep label and high heels. The height of elegance!

Smarmycreep had spent months buying ripped dust sheets covered in splodges of old paint. Wily painters and decorators had been busy finding old curtains and sheets for him and randomly throwing their dregs all over them. They were charging Smarmycreep a fortune and he was happy to pay handsomely for their smeared slime, filth and muck.

Smarmycreep had worked all year to launch his new range of clothes on the Ritz catwalk. He called it *Smarmcloaks*. He was determined to make his biggest, most sensational, splash, ever.

At last, the skeletal models appeared one-by-one and swaggered snootily down the catwalk. Each sported what looked like a long dog tail at the back of her head, as they showed off their *Smarmcloaks*. The audience gasped in amazement – and Mazik in amusement, recalling Goldie Wagtail.

The models gathered at the end of the catwalk and struck a dramatic, final pose to signal the climax of the show.

There was utter silence in the auditorium.

Nothing moved.

All eyes were focussed on the so-called *Queens of Fashion* sitting primly on the front row. Their expressions were completely vacant.

Then, suddenly, they began to touch their palms together in the most delicate applause.

The collection was a hit! The mindless audience *ooh'd* and *aah'd*. They'd never seen anything like *Smarmcloaks* before and decided they were the best thing, ever. They went wild!

Watching from the back so he could see both the show and the reactions of the audience, Spiky Smarmycreep grinned in triumph. Once again, he'd managed to win the favour of the fashion scene. Once again, he'd set a trend and, once again, he was on course to make another fortune, selling his designs to the rich and gullible.

The truth was that no one in the real world was the slightest bit impressed with Smarmycreep's designs. To them, he was just an empty-headed show-off, making fabulously expensive clothes for other empty-headed show-offs. Of course, Smarmycreep knew the truth, but *he* didn't care: as long as he made his money, what did it matter? In reality, he was sneaky, sly and totally two-faced.

He laughed all the way to the bank at the stick-insect models, the suckers in the audience, the absurd *Queens of Fashion*, the photographers fighting for the best shot, the fashion houses who slavishly followed his trendsetting and, especially, at the wealthy fools who actually bought his hugely expensive and utterly ridiculous, clothes. The more absurd the style, the more he charged and the more they lapped it up.

~

Mazik knew nothing of this. What he did know, was that he was utterly bored by the whole, ridiculous pantomime.

As the crowd erupted in wild applause, Mazik's patience suddenly snapped. He shut his eyes and muttered, 'Barnsley'. He opened them again and, as he did, he heard the audience shrieking in astonishment. There stood the models at the end of the catwalk. Each one was wearing a ridiculous *Smarmcloak* – all except for one. In the centre of the group stood the tallest and skinniest model of them all. In an instant, her *Smarmcloak* had vanished and, in its place, she was wearing Harmony's beautiful *fabar* dress.

Mazik looked across at Harmony. To her surprise and distaste, she was wearing the model's *Smarmcloak*!

The photographers clambered over each other to snap the model's fabulous outfit. As they did, the audience awoke from their mindless sleepwalk and cheered, wildly and, this time, genuinely.

Now high up in his private box, Smarmycreep exploded in fury, smashing the chairs and tables to the floor. His show had been hijacked, his year wasted; his moment of glory, ruined! The mysterious dress that appeared from nowhere, was going to capture the global headlines – headlines that should have belonged to him! The urge for revenge burned red hot in his heart.

As the models exited, vanishing into the darkness beyond the catwalk, Mazik shut his eyes and whispered, *'Barnsley'*. The *Smarmcloak* and the *fabar* dress switched back. Mazik breathed a sigh of relief.

But little did he know that his troubles were just beginning; Smarmycreep's security cameras had caught the exchange and it didn't take him long to identify the source of the shimmering dress.

~

The next few days were very uncomfortable for Spiky Smarmycreep.

Everyone thought that *he* was the one who had switched the outfits. Suddenly, there was a huge weight of expectation on his shoulders. The press were impatiently awaiting an announcement about the remarkable new material.

But he had no announcement to make.

As the days went by, the press began to speculate about the origin of the fabric. Some people even started to suggest that Smarmycreep was a fraud.

Smarmycreep's fury knew no bounds. He was a man of towering vanity and normally oblivious to criticism, but the *fabar* scandal was threatening his success.

He began to hatch a wicked plan to get even with the Sparks. He'd already made a mountain of money and didn't need to work. But someone had ruined his easy game. The Sparks had spoiled his hilarious fun and now he wanted revenge! He wanted it badly and he wanted it now!

He had no qualms about involving himself in petty crimes and wrongdoings. He'd started out in life with nothing and had no respect for the law. His secretive nature didn't permit him to trust anyone else to do exactly what he wanted and keep their trap shut. He would do his own dirty work.

~

Mazik had been practising his flying. Every morning, just before dawn, he would put on his Superhero onesie, slip on Gramps' hobnail boots as stabilisers and set off into the sky.

One morning, he decided to try flying to Jimmy's house. He packed a few essentials: his mobile, a pocket-knife, a length of sturdy string, a two-pence piece and six sheets of extra soft loo roll.

He set off early, keeping himself amused by tracking one of the neighbourhood foxes and her cubs and listening to the local bats and owls.

As the house came into view, Mazik was shocked to see all the lights blazing. The front door was swinging in the breeze and he could see that it was broken and hanging by the top hinge. Mazik was about to land, when someone dressed in black came running out. The figure threw something into the saddlebags on either side of his bicycle's back wheel and rode off at top speed.

Mazik was momentarily torn between checking on Jimmy and Harmony, or chasing the thief.

He decided to fly after the bike – although he had no idea what he would do if he caught up with it.

He quickly flew ahead of his quarry. Then, still floating in the black of night, he turned to face the rapidly oncoming cyclist.

Suddenly, Mazik screamed straight towards the cyclist's face.

The thief shrieked in terror when he saw the oncoming, flying figure. The bike wobbled and bounced off the kerb, but, somehow, he managed to regain his balance and cycled on like a maniac.

Mazik turned and charged him from behind, planting Gramps' hobnail boots firmly up the villain's backside.

The thief somersaulted over the handlebars and he felt he was in a slow-motion horror movie, as his unprotected head cracked hard against the edge of a kerbstone and the bike crashed down on top of him.

He lay there, unconscious, blood trickling from a ragged scar on his forehead, while Mazik opened the two saddlebags and recovered the stolen swag.

Then he flew back to Jimmy's house and landed outside the front door. He peered in, anxiously and looked around. There, roped to the hall radiator, were Jimmy and Harmony, with their mouths taped.

Mazik took out his pocketknife and cut the ropes.

Jimmy ripped off the tape and gasped, 'We've just been burgled!' He checked that Harmony was unharmed.

'Am I pleased to see you, Mazik!' said Jimmy, 'But what are you doing here?'

Mazik held up the two objects. 'Look what I found outside! What are they?'

Harmony smiled, 'They're the priceless rocks we brought back from *Paulinus 627* and the Moon!'

'You found them outside, Mazik?' asked Jimmy.

'Yes. There's a man with a bike, out there. I think he's had a crash.'

Jimmy went out and looked down the road in the dawn light. He spotted a dark figure in the gutter, slumped against the kerb, alongside a bike. Mazik came out with his mobile torch app and they went to have a look. The figure was breathing, but motionless.

'What shall we do, Jimmy?'

'Let's tie him up,' said Jimmy.

Mazik pulled the string from his pocket. 'This'll do for now.' He leant forward and tied the thief's nose-ring to the grate his face was lying on.

'You're a very resourceful young chap,' said Jimmy. Mazik brimmed with pride. 'What else have you got in your pockets?'

Mazik switched his mobile to camera and took a photo of the burglar.

'Anything else?'

Mazik put his hand in his pocket and pulled out a wad of loo paper. Suddenly blurting 'I need this *now*!' he darted back to Jimmy's house.

Harmony had been on the phone to the local police station. Luckily, their friend DCI Vera Smidgley was on early shift.

'Hi Vera; Harmony, here.'

'If it's a Spark, it's trouble!' laughed Vera.

'We've been burgled, but Mazik has found what was stolen, outside.'

'And what *was* stolen?' asked Vera. 'No, let me guess – the Moon rocks!'

'And our rocks from the asteroid.'

'Oh, a priceless haul – and a tempting target! Are you okay?'

'We were tied up and gagged, but we're alright.'

'Aggravated burglary. Do you have a description of the burglar?'

At that moment, Mazik raced back in. 'We've got him. Better call an ambulance!'

Vera overheard. 'I'm onto it; I'll call them. I'll be there shortly, too.'

As Vera drove up, she saw Jimmy in his dressing gown and Mazik in his Superhero onesie – elegantly offset by the huge, hobnail boots.

They were standing over a man in black, who seemed to be praying to the god of the underworld. He had a nasty gash on his forehead. A line of blood flowed round his nose ring, along the string and into the drain.

'Fascinating! How very novel,' said Vera slapping the handcuffs on him and taking a few photographs. 'I'm DCI Smidgley. I'm arresting you for aggravated burglary. Anything you say may be used as evidence in court. What's your name, sir?'

'Scumbag!' the man shouted, 'Filthy Scumbag!'

'Right, Mr Scumbag,' said Vera. 'Is that 'Scumbag' with two b's, or just the one?'

'Filthy Scumbag!' he shrieked again.

Vera looked at Mazik. 'Perhaps he's calling for his friends in the sewers.'

'Or the god of the grate!' said Mazik.

Vera inspected the bike closely. 'Excuse me, Mr Scumbag, is this your bicycle?'

'Geroff me bike, Pig!'

'Regrettably, I have to inform you that it isn't your bike. It was reported stolen, late last night.

I'll add that to the charge sheet. Are there any more offences you'd like me to take into account?'

Me head's down the bog!
Get me out!
Pig!
Sow!
Stupid old cow!

Just then, the ambulance arrived. The thief was cut free and released from the handcuffs. He struggled aboard, the blow to his head scrambling his attempts to shout 'Scumbag'.

Scambug!
Mugscab!
Bugmasc!
Evil-smelling gasbum!

He was driven to A&E at High Woodley General, to have his wounds stitched and his language repaired. He was released without revealing his true identity and avoided being spotted by the press.

Jimmy and Harmony didn't press charges, as the rocks were recovered and they thought the thief had suffered enough. But what they didn't realise was that the precious rocks weren't the real target of his raid. That still lay scrunched up and undiscovered in the bottom of his pocket. Of course, what Vera and the Sparks didn't know was that the thief was, in fact, the odious Spiky Smarmycreep, himself!

~

'Would you like to come in for a cup of tea, Vera?' asked Jimmy.

'I wouldn't say no, thanks; my shift has just finished. It had been quite uneventful, until you sparked some excitement. I was just starting to miss your calls. Perhaps Mazik will take over from where Jammy Jimmy left off, when he became such a distinguished, international celebrity.'

'Less of the 'celebrity' nonsense, if you please! I'm still the same old Jimmy!'

'Now Mazik, how come you found these precious Moon rocks outside Jimmy and Harmony's house? Was it a sleepover? You were awoken by the commotion of the burglary, came down to find the criminal had tied up Jimmy and Harmony, fallen off his bike in his panic to flee and dropped the rocks?' Vera was hoping that Mazik would take the simple route and just nod his head in agreement.

'No,' blurted Mazik, without thinking.

He realised he'd been too hasty and played for time. 'My sister, Annie, used to call you "Defective Specky Very Smudgley"! Is that right?'

'I've been promoted: it's DCI now. "Defective Cheese Specky Very Smudgley." Anyway, what do you mean, *"No*?"'

'I mean…er…that's right,' fibbed Mazik. 'Except I took the rocks out of his saddlebags myself.'

Vera laughed heartily. 'He was a sight to cheer the heart of a weary, old copper. I'll add it to the stories I'm going to write when I retire!'

She finished her cup of tea and turned to Jimmy and Harmony. 'Right, if you two can make statements at High Woodley Police Station in the next few days, I'll process the paperwork and keep you informed. Bye!'

Vera was inclined to agree that the thief had received his punishment. She had more pressing matters to attend to.

Once Vera had left, Jimmy turned to Mazik. 'Who are you kidding, Mazik? What were you really doing here before dawn?'

Harmony put her arm around Mazik. 'He was doing what he said. Leave him alone, Jimmy. I'm very grateful that he rescued us from that horrid thief! Well done Mazik!'

That sent a warm tingle of pride through Mazik. She winked at him and said, 'Hadn't you better fly home, before your Mum discovers you've disappeared?'

Mazik ran to the broken front door, but it was getting light outside, now and there was traffic on the road. 'Can you give me a lift home, please, Dimmy?' yawned Mazik.

They jumped into Jimmy's car and, a couple of minutes later, Jimmy dropped Mazik outside his house. Jimmy gave Mazik a quizzical look, but Mazik darted out and shut the car door before he could be interrogated. He quickly checked that nobody could see and flew straight in through his bedroom window, landing just as his Mum came in to see why he hadn't got up yet.

'What are you doing in that old Superhero onesie, Mazik? Aren't those Gramps' dirty old hobnail boots? What on earth are you wearing

90

those for? I hope you didn't sleep in them?'

''Course not! Anyway, they're clean.' He raised the soles to show her. 'I was having a space game. I'm a lunar astronaut, like Jimmy. I have to wear these in zero gravity, so that I don't just fly through the window!'

'You're as bonkers as Gramps! Breakfast is on the table. You're late. You'll have to fly!'

Chapter 7

Whoosh!

What Gramps hadn't realised, when he'd confiscated the *Hot Headers* tin, was that Mazik could still make more *QuanTum* capsules whenever he pleased. He just had to

squeeze and press
squash and push
squinch and pinch
squelch and belch

and a smooth compact cylinder appeared in his belly button, waiting to be unplugged. A very satisfactory process. In fact, a most agreeable, delightful sensation, indeed.

It occurred to Mazik that perhaps he could use the *QuanTum* paste at school. A little dab on sneaky Samantha's nose, to stop her telling porkies; a sprinkle in the piano teacher's gloves, to make her pointy fingers even longer; a smattering around the rim of the headteacher's hat, to make his head bigger still. He thought of his teachers: Mr Hand, Mrs Foot, Miss Cheek, Mr Chinn, Miss Lipp and the classroom assistant, Richard Winkle.

He scratched his nose. He scratched his left ear. He scratched his right knee. As he rubbed an eye he was struck by a worrying thought. He'd been producing *QuanTum* for some time, now. He'd first swallowed it on impulse and, if he was honest, he'd never really thought about the consequences. If he'd accidentally got some *QuanTum* paste on his skin, he'd now be a hideously lopsided, Frankenstein's monster, creeping out of the cellar to frighten all the children! Digesting it no longer seemed to affect him physically, but might it be changing him in some more subtle way? Perhaps it would be best, after all, if *QuanTum's* amazing energy stayed in the vegetable plot.

He lay on his bed and remembered his trip into space with Yorke. He'd somehow been infected with Yorke's strange, alien ways: whirring his eyes, producing powerful *QuanTum* capsules, rearranging things and flying. He now called these strange powers *Quasies* But surely, there were no more surprises! There just couldn't be!

Suddenly, he felt that thrilling power surge through his body again: *Yorke's spark.*

He stretched out to gather his duvet close, for comfort. He felt round for it, but it wasn't there.

He looked around.

No duvet! No pillow! No bed!

He was lying on the floor in Gramps' study! Gramps' exercise weights were on one side of him and a pile of mouldy books about coins were on the other.

How did he get here? How would he get home unseen? Once again, he had the troubling thought that it wasn't merely having swallowed *QuanTum*, but the way he made more of the stuff that was the problem. He'd promised himself no more mix-and-match part exchange like happened on the train, but the power had evolved and turned inwards, so that it was he who was disappearing and reappearing randomly.

Gramps was at his desk, typing on his computer keyboard.

'Er, Gramps?' whispered Mazik. Gramps nearly jumped out of his skin. His chair crashed backwards, cushioned by the stack of mouldy coin books.

'What the blinkin' ummers! What's tha doin' here at this time of night?'

'Is everything alright, dear?' shouted Grandma from downstairs 'I heard a crash!'

'Fine, dear! I just tripped over a pile of old books!'

'I've *told* you to declutter. I'll find you dead under a heap of festering coin books, one fine day!'

'Yes, dear! As long as one of them is Abramson's *Early Pennies*, it'll be a fine way to die!' He turned back to Mazik. 'What is tha doin' here, lad?' he whispered. 'How am ah goin' to get thee back home? Tha's turned into one of them cartoon characters from comics!'

'Soz, Gramps. I don't know what happened. I think I'd better fly home before I'm missed.'

'Well, what is this new *thing*? Feels like we've bin here before. Mazik's latest disaster!'

'I don't know. Perhaps the flying and disappearing things have developed into a space-time shift – instant transportation! I'd better go.'

Mazik climbed onto Gramps' desk to leave by the window. 'Goodnight, Gramps.'

'Aye, tek care, lad. Try and master new *thing*. Tha'll get the hang of it, if tha thinks about it. Good night!'

Mazik cautiously flew off.

'I should write a book about thee!' muttered Gramps. He shut the window seconds before Grandma came in to investigate.

'Just look at the clutter in here. First thing in the morning, you can take these piles of useless, old books to High Woodley tip!'

'Some of them's worth a fortune, our lass!' complained Gramps.

'Well, keep those and throw the others out! When did you last read any of them?'

'They're reference books. Useful to have on hand, tha knows!'

'Just get rid of them. They're a danger to life and limb and a fire hazard, Obadiah Spark! First thing!'

'First thing!' echoed Gramps. He waited until she'd gone downstairs. 'First thing after next Blue Moon!' he muttered.

~

The following night, Mazik tied his wrist to the bedpost, thinking that may prevent him from flying off. But as he fell asleep, he felt a powerful tugging sensation, as if some force were trying to pull him away. He resisted and held on grimly. The force gradually weakened, then faded away.

The next night, Mazik was sure that he could hang on and stay where he was, if he really wanted. He didn't tie his wrist to the bedpost, but, when the force came, he went as rigid as he could, until it had weakened. Then he relaxed.

Whoosh!

Without warning, he found himself in the summerhouse. He opened the door and quietly crept back up the stairs, to his own room. Luckily, nobody noticed him – even though he'd grabbed a packet of chocolate biscuits as he tiptoed through the kitchen.

He now knew the range of the force. A full blast would carry him a kilometre to Grandma and Gramps'. A mild bout would take him a few dozen metres into the garden. Instantly.

~

Over the next week, Mazik practised the space-time shift. If he focussed hard, he could control when it happened and how far he could travel. By imagining a scene in his head, he could fix exactly where he was going. He picked up a magazine photograph of the Niagara Falls as he set the stopwatch on his bedside digital clock: 1...2...3...

Whoosh!

The noise of pounding water, cascading in huge torrents over the edge of the mighty falls, was deafening. It was an amazing sight. He was so close he was soaked by the spray. He zoomed out to where he could see the full length of the waterfall and wasn't being drenched or deafened. He tried to chase the rainbow, but it was always just out of reach. He looked down and saw the cruise boats circling in the spray. There were crowds of people on the viewing platforms, taking photographs. He hovered over the scene for a good while, but he felt his wet clothes getting cold. He brought the image of his bedroom into mind and

Whoosh!

He leapt off his bed, thinking he was wet through. He looked at his stopwatch. It had just clicked over to 4...5...6. Remarkable! No time had passed, but he *was* soaked through. He changed out of the wet clothes and left them in a heap on the bedroom floor. Mum would probably clear them up, sometime.

He picked up his mobile. 'Er, Gramps?'

'Mr Trouble?'

'Er, Gramps. Are you home? I'm coming over to show you something.'

'Hang on while ah nail furniture t'floor, shave mi head, put Goldie Wagtail in kennel and start mi pacemaker! Right, lad, ah'm now braced for onslaught!'

'Are you in your study?'

'Aye, lad. Is tha bringin' tha...'

Whoosh!

Spontaneously, Mazik appeared right in front of Gramps' nose, '...football cards?' Gramps stopped abruptly, 'Crikey! Tha startled me summat terrible. Ah'll have to sit down while mi heart recovers. Tha'll be death of uz, tha daft, young tyke! Will tha stop givin' uz shocks? Is tha tryin' to inherit early, or summat?'

'Who are you talking to, Obie?' shouted Grandma from the hall.

'It's just uz radio. Ah'll turn volume down.' Then Gramps whispered, 'So, tha's mastered new skill, young man?'

'Yes, Gramps. I just think of a place, or look at a photo and, I'm there instantly.'

'For how long?'

'Until I think of home. But when I get home, no time has passed. I've timed it on my stopwatch.'

'Another of Yorke Barnsley's little stunts!?'

'Well, it has to be the last! It just *has* to be! We'll have to find a way to stop it, before I go bonkers, Gramps!'

'Even more bonkers, tha means. This one's trickiest. Tha's bound to get in t'trouble, lad!'

'I'll try not to! I'm going home, now. Bye Gramps!' And he was gone as abruptly as he'd appeared.

Chapter 8

Spiky Spiked

Spiky Smarmycreep had not the slightest interest in Jimmy's Moon rocks. He didn't give a damn for such things.

What Smarmycreep had really been after, he now caressed in his hands. Its silky-smooth warmth radiated such an exciting sensation. As he entwined it between his fingers, his eyes closed and he dreamed of golden beaches kissed by a sparkling blue sea.

His real aim during the raid had been to get some *fabar* from Harmony's dress. He'd been quick and stealthy: he'd taken just a ribbon, avoided any damage and replaced the dress, with great care. He didn't want to raise suspicion.

Since the fashion show, photographs of Harmony's fabulous dress had been on the front cover of every fashion magazine in the world. Smarmycreep had soon recovered from the physical battering Mazik had dealt him, but the embarrassment had not gone away. The indignation, the sheer humiliation of defeat in the gutter by a child, his nose tied to the drain, burned red hot atop the fire of envy, over the *fabar* dress stealing the show.

He swore that he would have his revenge. He'd fathom the secrets of *fabar*. Smarmycreep had never seen anything like its shimmering iridescence. He knew his fashion ideas were worthless and vulgar compared to *fabar's* subtlety and versatility. He'd hoped to steal the idea; discover what the material was; learn to make it; ramp up production; conquer the market; and bask in global glory. But the fabric in his hands was beyond his understanding and just fuelled his hatred and envy.

His mind turned to destruction.

He took his most lurid, wretched *Smarmcloak*, fashioned it into a long dark cloak with a hood and rode the underground to High Woodley. He'd found Amy Spark's address without difficulty and would hit the Sparks in their most vulnerable spot.

He prowled the area, searching for Mazik.

Mazik had just come out of the house, with Chepi on a lead and a dog-ball thrower in his hand. They were walking towards Golden Arch Park.

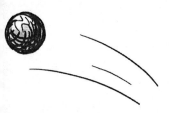

When they arrived, Mazik released Chepi and started using the catapult to fling the ball, much further than he could throw by himself. Chepi rushed after it and didn't mind if it went in the heather on the rough moorland at the top of the park. He'd snaffle around in the undergrowth until he'd found it – or some other dog's ball – and come rushing back, wagging his tail furiously.

Mazik gave the catapult an especially hard heave and the ball arced high over the moor, into the dark woods beyond. Chepi watched the flight of the ball and, as it reached its apex, went rushing after it into the dense woodland. When he didn't come back straight away, Mazik thought the ball must have stuck in a thicket, but he couldn't hear Chepi barking. He whistled loudly and waited.

Still no Chepi.

Mazik walked towards the forest and hesitantly entered where Chepi had rushed in. There was nothing to be seen. No Chepi. No ball.

Nothing.

A dark, hooded figure – with a freshly-scarred forehead and sores where his nose ring had pulled – had lured the little dog with a bone, scooped him into a sack and run off under cover of the dark wood. Inside the sack, Chepi whimpered in fright.

'Chepi! Chepi! Chepi!' Mazik shouted. He ran around, feeling increasingly worried and on the verge of panic. He phoned home.

'Has Chepi come back home without me? I can't find him anywhere! I threw the ball into the woods, but he's nowhere to be seen.'

'We'll come and help you search. I'll bring Mum,' said Annie.

A few minutes later he heard them calling across the moor. As they approached, they could tell from Mazik's slumped shoulders that Chepi was still lost. They fanned out through the woods and searched for an hour before returning home.

Annie posted details of Chepi on the *Lost Dogs* website and made some posters to put round Golden Arch Park.

Mazik was heartbroken.

He climbed into bed, put the duvet over his head and wept into his pillow.

When he awoke, there was a message on his mobile:

*Kill the fabric, kid
or the dog dies!*

Below was a photograph of Chepi looking scared.

Mazik rushed down to show it to Amy and Annie. Of course, they didn't know about Yorke Barnsley, or where *fabar* really came from. Even so, they decided he should forward the message to DCI Vera Smidgley, with an explanation and to Jimmy, who, it seemed to Mazik, knew everybody in the world – and beyond! Mazik also forwarded it to Gramps and Grandma.

Jimmy passed the message onto his friend and fellow astronaut, Julie Hardman.

Julie was a computer whizz and she started tracking the mobile from which it had been sent. It took her less than two minutes to send Jimmy a name: Spiky Smarmycreep!

She was disgusted at the thought of the odious little toe-rag and his ridiculous *Smarmcloaks*. 'Mr Obnoxious!' she muttered.

Vera Smidgley soon found a security video, from High Woodley underground station, of a tall, mean-faced figure in a dark-hooded *Smarmcloak.*

'Positive ID, High Woodley tube station. Definitely Smarmycreep!' she emailed Jimmy and the others. Vera organised search parties and the local dogwalkers all came out to help.

It was only now that Mazik went back to the photograph of Chepi attached to the threatening message he'd received. A terrible thought flashed into Mazik's head: *Where did Smarmycreep get the dog tails for his catwalk models?* He looked hard at Chepi and suddenly realised how to use his powers...

Whoosh!

...there he was, right next to Chepi's basket in Smarmycreep's posh City apartment! Chepi looked up and launched himself onto Mazik, pinning him to the floor and licking his face all over.

Smarmycreep was standing in his smart kitchen, listening to music on the other side of the open-plan penthouse suite. He was a heavy metal fan and the air was filled with the sound of pounding music. He had his back to them, but heard Chepi yelping and was about to look round. Mazik was absolutely certain that if he was caught, or even just seen, not only would Chepi's life be in jeopardy, but his as well.

He now needed his *Quasies* – his powers – at full strength or he was doomed. He shut his eyes tightly, held Chepi firmly, drummed *Barnsley! Barnsley!* in his head and pictured his bedroom.

Whoosh!

Instantly, they were bouncing on his bed, Chepi scragging the bedclothes and barking.

Mazik blew a sigh of relief and sprinted downstairs. 'Chepi's come home! Chepi's escaped! Look!'

Chepi came rushing down the stairs, did a double roll on the slippery floor at the bottom and leapt up as everyone fussed over him.

Feed me! Feed me! he barked excitedly in doggy speak. *This must be worth a ton of extra biscuits!*

~

In spite of Chepi's joyful return, dognapping was a serious crime and DCI Vera Smidgley was on the warpath. She detested the likes of Smarmycreep. She hated the fact that he thought he could do as he pleased – threatening children and kidnapping pets! Vera wouldn't stand for it.

She was now approaching his apartment to arrest him under the Law Against Odious Toerags.

Little did she know, however, that someone else was also on their way to visit Smarmycreep.

Mazik had found a sponge ball from the Gutterball game, put on a pair of rubber gloves and thoroughly drenched the ball in *QuanTum* paste from his *Hot Headers* tin.

Once the ball was soaked, he pictured Smarmycreep's apartment in his head and...

Whoosh!

...there he was!

Smarmycreep had realised that Chepi had escaped and he was out searching the neighbourhood.

By the time he returned, Mazik was gone. *Something* had been left behind, though: Smarmycreep saw the squidgy sponge ball in Chepi's basket. He assumed that Chepi had it in his mouth when he was captured. It would be ideal for smearing onto a new *Smarmcloak*. He picked it up and squeezed it. The paste ran all over his hands.

Without thinking, he wiped his hands dry on his arms and scratched his nose and ears. He rubbed an eye and swept his fingers through his hair.

The doorbell rang. Smarmycreep looked through the spyhole. 'Who's there? No street scum! Clear off!'

'Detective Chief Inspector Smidgley, Mr Smarmycreep. Please open the door.'

She heard a series of bolts and latches being unlocked and then the door cracked open an inch. 'Yeah, what do you want, copper!?'

'I'm investigating the disappearance of a small boy's pet dog!'

'Haven't you better things to do? Don't waste my valuable time.'

'Open the door,' said Vera firmly, 'I insist!'

'Pig! Sow! Stupid old cow!'

The refrain gave Vera a cold shiver of familiarity. 'Being offensive won't help,' she said. 'I could charge you with obstructing the course of justice. I strongly advise you to cooperate.'

Just then, she heard a deep, rumbling groan. It sounded like approaching thunder.

Aaaahhhggggg!

screamed Smarmycreep violently, as the door creaked slowly open.

Vera peered in and was startled by the horrific scene. Smarmycreep's hair looked like a large bush perched on his head. His ears hung down to his shoulders. His nose was a foot long and he had one grossly bulging eye. Each hand was the size of a bucket, on an arm that stretched to the ground.

For someone so vain and showy, it was shattering.

'I feel terrible,' he growled. 'I think I'm ill. I must have caught something from that filthy hound... Oh, blast! I've said it now!' His arms were now too heavy to carry. He sank to the floor, cradled himself in anguish and started to whimper pathetically.

Just then, Vera's mobile buzzed with a text from Mazik: 'Chepi's come home! He just came back!'

Vera was baffled: she'd expected to find Chepi at Smarmycreep's apartment. How had Chepi got all the way to High Woodley so quickly? *Of course, being a Spark,* reasoned Vera, *Chepi could probably have bought his own ticket at the tube station and caught the train home!*

She looked at the pathetic state Smarmycreep was in and thought, *Well, if Chepi and Mazik are safe, there's no point in arresting Smarmycreep. It looks like he's been punished enough. Anyway, I'd never get him into the police car, with his head so big and arms that long.*

As she called for an ambulance, she had a moment of *déjà vu.*

She shook it out of her head. 'That's all for now, sir. The ambulance will be here shortly. Please don't get up; I'll let myself out.' As she was leaving, she added as an afterthought, 'Oh, by the way, I recommend you put a *Smarmcloak* over your head when you go out. You don't want to frighten the children.'

'Look at my hands! Looks at my nose! I'm wrecked, I'm ruined, I'm revolting! I'm repugnant!'

'Indeed,' agreed Vera, without sympathy. 'You always were. I recommend you avoid mirrors!'

He was carried off screaming and snivelling in pain, with a *Smarmcloak* draped over him to hide his head and body. The ambulance crew took him to an isolation room at High Woodley General Hospital. There, he was sedated, while surgeons urgently debated how to restore him to normal.

Chapter 9

Sparkling Hues

Mazik decided he deserved a sleepover at his grandparents'. He phoned, 'Grandma, can I stay over, tonight? I'll bring my football cards!'

'Yes, of course. Have you asked Mum?'

'Oh, I forgot. I'll get her to phone you.'

In the morning, Mazik awoke at 5:58 and stood outside his grandparents' bedroom door, knowing Gramps would appear at any second. At precisely 6:00, Gramps crept out, bent forward and peered into Mazik's face in the dim morning light. Then, they silently tiptoed into Mazik's room.

Gramps reached over to the bedside light and touched the base a couple of times to make it brighter. He looked closely at Mazik, 'Did tha wash last night, Mazik?'

'Yes, of course I did,' fibbed Mazik.

'When did tha turn blue, lad?'

Mazik gave Gramps a look of disbelief, but he recalled feeling both *Yorke's spark* and a peculiar *QuanTummy* sensation during the night. He remembered the selfie he'd taken on Yorke's spacecraft, when his face appeared Earth-coloured. He also remembered the weird colours he'd turned, on first swallowing *QuanTum*. He went to the washbasin and switched on the mirror light. 'Oh no! My face has turned electric blue! Just like Yorke Barnsley! What'll I do, Gramps?' He pulled his pyjama jacket up, with his blue hands, to show his chest was blue, then stretched his elastic waistband and looked down. 'Oh no!' His feet were blue, as well. 'It's all that Yorke's fault! I've got a swimming lesson at school today. I can't go blue all over!'

'Same colour as water – we won't be able to see thee!' chuckled Gramps. 'Don't worry, ah'll phone and tell them tha's off colour!'

'It's not funny, Gramps! Grandma will go crazy! What'll Mum say? I can't go to school, blue!'

'Perhaps it'll wear off. Let's go and have breakfast. Tha can have *blue*berry jam on tha toast!'

'Gramps!'

~

As Mazik relished the delicious toast, rainbow colours swept over his body.

'Tha's Richard of York – red, orange and yeller!'

Mazik rushed to the downstairs cloakroom, to look in the mirror and moaned. 'Gave Battle In Vain!'

He went back to finish breakfast, then the electric blue shade returned.

'Tha knows this is another little habit tha's picked up from that chap from Barnsley!'

'Yorke. I know!' Mazik looked close to tears.

'Well then, tha knows what tha mus' do. Shut tha eyes and think of Barnsley! Space, not place!'

'Okay. Hang on!' He shut his eyes, pictured the spaceman and said to himself: *Yorke Barnsley, it's not funny!*

He opened his eyes. Gramps had brought in a mirror. 'Tha's a little less blue, now, lad. I can see patches of natural, coming through.'

'Ooo, yes, I've got freckly cheeks and blue hair. I could form a punk band!'

'Try again, see if tha can get rid of blue hue.'

Mazik screwed up his eyes. 'Think natural, son,' encouraged Gramps. 'Oo, tha's gradually turnin' normal. Where's tha swimmin' lesson?'

'At Yellowfield Pool.'

'Oh, no! That's blown it!'

Mazik opened his eyes and looked in the mirror. Now, his face was yellow; his hair, blue; his forehead...a greenish mix.

'Ah'd best shut mi trap,' said Gramps, apologetically.

Mazik shut his eyes and repeated, *Barnsley. Barnsley. Barnsley,* in his head.

He was too scared to open his eyes. 'What's happening, Gramps?'

'We're getting there! Oh yes, look in mirror, lad!'

Mazik plucked up the courage to look. 'Phew! Normal! Ring my bell!'

'What a very strange thing to say!' said Grandma, who had just bustled into the kitchen. 'I hope you're not becoming as barmy as your Gramps. Do have some more toast – there's plenty where that came from. You can have jam. We have redcurrant or blackcurrant or greengage, or orange marmalade. Oh, I see we've got blueberry jam, too. Which do you want?'

'Er, do you have some honey?'

'Good choice!' said Gramps. 'Ah have honey, every mornin'. Double, if ah'm off colour!' he chortled. 'Tha can have cherry yoghurt, if tha fancies.' Gramps winked at Mazik and went off to the bathroom, chuckling and singing to himself.

A few moments later, Gramps galloped back into the kitchen. His face was electric blue! 'Ah think it's catchin'!'

'Obadiah Spark, you silly old fool!' shouted Grandma. 'Go and wash it off immediately! What do you think you look like!?'

Gramps went back upstairs and Mazik followed him into his study.

''Appen it's catchin'. Ah call it *contagious colouration!*'

'Picture yourself in the shaving mirror, Gramps.' Gramps shut his eyes and thought, *Barnsley.* 'No good, son, nowt 'appened! Ah'll just have to get a guitar and sing Rhythm and Blues.'

They looked at each other for a few seconds. Gradually, Gramps returned to his usual tone, but Mazik went blue.

'Oh no! We've swapped colours!' said Mazik.

''Ecky thump, ah've never known owt like it! It's all fault of that blithering Yorke Barnsley! Interferin' alien! And tha big brother Jimmy, flouncin' off into space and bringin' back *intergalactic infectation!*' complained Gramps.

'I don't think it's Jimmy's fault, Gramps,' said Mazik, thinking of his *QuanTum* diet. 'Anyway, what's an *intergalactic infectation?*'

'Ah dunno, summat bad ah just med up!'

Mazik picked up a photograph. It was of the wedding of Jimmy and Harmony's friends, Julie Patel and Tom Hardman. They were married on the asteroid they'd flown to: *Paulinus 627*. Rick Hudson, the international rugby player, and Amanda Heavenly completed the crew of six. Reflecting the different-coloured faces in the photo, Mazik was now pulsing alternate shades of pink and brown. 'It's gone berserk, Gramps! Hadn't we better get a proper doctor?'

"Appen we ought. We'd best show Grandma Lucy. There's no disguisin' it now, lad.'

Grandma was sitting at the breakfast table, reading *Green News*. She'd turned a vivid shade of green!

Gramps said soothingly, 'Now don't get alarmed our lass, but best look at thysen in mirror.'

He held up the hand mirror.

Grandma screamed. Then she looked at Mazik, pulsing pink and brown and screamed again. She was now green with increasingly wide bands of crimson, as she got angrier.

'Now, calm thysen. It's nowt serious,' said Gramps, trying to avoid a volcanic eruption. 'Just a touch of *contagious colouration*, our lass. Best visit Doctor Black.' Her crimson bands turned black.

Gramps gestured soothingly for Grandma to calm down, as they looked at each other for a few seconds. 'There, see tha's fine now. Same as ever.'

'But *you're* going green!' she replied, her voice wavering in alarm. Gramps and Mazik sat silently contemplating the word *Barnsley* with their eyes shut and after a minute they had all returned to their natural complexions.

~

Mazik had managed to avoid all the excitement about Jimmy and Harmony's wedding. They'd tried to keep the event quiet, but inevitably it leaked into the press and was reported widely.

On the big day, Mazik, as ring bearer, walked down the aisle behind Jimmy and his best man, Rick Hudson. Mazik's big sister, Annie and Rick's girlfriend, the saxophonist Amanda Heavenly, were bridesmaids.

Harmony arrived suitably late, allowing the excitement to build.

When she did appear, the intake of breath was audible. She looked sensational in her scintillating, iridescent, *fabar* wedding dress. The attendees broke into spontaneous applause, before the celebrant politely called them to order.

Everything was going to plan until Mazik turned to face the assembly. He'd worked hard at controlling the feelings of *QuanTummy* and was certain that he'd got control of his powers in time for the big day, which he was excited about despite his unquelled sibling envy.

Mazik had been keeping a close eye on the ring, a gold band with a large diamond, to make sure it didn't slip off the plush velvet cushion.

Rick was whispering to Jimmy that he'd only just got back in time, from visiting his grandparents – in Barnsley.

As soon as Mazik heard 'Barnsley', he erupted internally with *Yorke's spark* and pulsating *QuanTummy* and then his face turned sparkling gold! His dimples glowed. His eyes twinkled. The assembly gasped.

The magic spread instantly. Annie turned electric blue, which clashed with her bridesmaid's dress. Rick looked at his girlfriend, Amanda. He turned brown and she turned pink. Jimmy exchanged glances with his business partner, Dizzy: they exchanged colours, too. Dizzy's husband, the pop idol, Lazy J, looked at Harmony and went pink. Harmony glowed brown.

In fact, it wasn't long before everybody had changed colour. At first, they all stared in astonishment. But then someone started giggling and, before long, it was general pandemonium. The confusion only increased when Mazik's single colours started to blend in astonishing multicoloured, moving patterns and this almost immediately spread to everyone else.

After a few minutes of laughter, the wedding celebrant again called order and reminded them that it was a serious occasion. Her face was a feast of emerald pop art, with flashes of diamond to match the ring.

The wedding photographer was briefly distracted by the swirling whirlpools spinning around the skin on his arms. But he uploaded the scene onto the internet while Jimmy and Harmony were signing the register.

Jimmy was about to explode with fury at Mazik, but was immediately hypnotized by the shimmering pinpoints of multicoloured light shining out of Mazik's mass of cheeky freckles. Each one was a different colour, with spotlights gleaming from his dimples. His colours reflected and shimmered on the wall.

~

It went viral in minutes.

Offscreen someone pleaded: 'A sink? A sink!' They'd wanted to try to wash it off, but the misheard name stuck – *async*.

Everyone wanted *async* and they didn't have to wait long. Mazik's *async* swept around the whole world with the rising sun. Complexions popped and fizzed beyond control. It was a global riot of ever-changing colours: everybody equally unique.

Warfare ended; people were having too much fun with *async* and, with differences less obvious, they lost the will to fight. Peace broke out.

With images of Mazik's freckly dimples now spread around the entire globe, he had a thrill of excitement. He'd done something that gained the sort of respect that Jimmy received. But he still knew that what Jimmy had achieved owed nothing to any superpower: he'd done it all with his own native wit, or with help from his friends; Mazik's quest to move out of Jimmy's shadow was still a distant dream.

~

After his first day back at school after the excitement of the wedding, Mazik strolled with his grandparents to the Green Café. Lots of students were passing between the neighbouring university and the *Revolution!* sports arena. Mazik was recognised immediately and people – of all colours of the rainbow – waved and shouted. He waved back and laughed at the spectacular patterns and explosions of colour, shimmering on their faces.

One boy accidentally bumped into a passing girl. He turned to her to apologise but his face flared like a firework display. She ran off, giggling, with splashes of crimson washing over her.

Waves of colour rippled through the throng. When groups were laughing or talking excitedly, the colours were bright with lots of glittery explosions. Where clusters of people were more serious, the tones were muted, with far fewer bursts of colours or patterns.

They entered the café and ordered food and drinks. Grandma picked up a copy of the latest *Green News* and didn't know or care that varying shades of green swept over her face, depending on the article she was reading. Her skin changed from artichoke to avocado, olive to jade, then sea green to mint. She rather liked the idea of being a green granny.

Chapter 10

Gobstoppers

As soon as Jimmy returned from his honeymoon, he rushed around to see Mazik and started the usual wrestle. But, instead of fighting back, Mazik just went limp and lifeless. This wasn't the normal response that Jimmy expected. 'What's the matter, Little Man?'

'You!' replied Mazik, sullenly.

'But, I've specially come to see you. What's the problem?'

'Everything's perfect for you and it's all going haywire for me.'

'Haywire?' queried Jimmy, frowning deeply. 'Well, I have been meaning to ask you about a few, strange things, recently.'

'I know,' replied Mazik, morosely.

'Like the episode with the Moon rock thief and the thing that happened on the catwalk and the message you beamed onto the wall at the wedding. And I've heard rumours that Smarmycreep is seriously ill, in isolation. What's going on, Mazik?'

'I don't even know where to start.' Mazik sounded deflated.

'I see,' said Jimmy, thinking what a challenge fatherhood might be. 'The beginning's usually a good place. Though, I know about *Qua* and *fabar* and you've already told me about the space flight with Yorke, so take it from there. How about we walk down to the Ice Cream Parlour and you tell me all about it on the way?'

As they set off, Mazik asked, 'How am I ever going to be anything but Jimmy Spark's stupid, kid brother?' His chin quivered, he was so upset. He tried to hide it behind his hand.

'C'mon Mazik, share your troubles,' said Jimmy, reassuringly putting an arm around Mazik's shoulders. 'Nothing's ever as bad as it seems.'

Mazik tried to explain all the *Quasies* that seemed to result from *Yorke's spark* or swallowing *QuanTum*. He wasn't sure which of these was the cause, just that it all somehow originated from *Qua*. 'It's all hopelessly out of control. I'm a one-person disaster zone!'

'You've done far more than I ever achieved at your age.'

'Rubbish!' protested Mazik, crossly.

'It's true!' said Jimmy, earnestly. 'Some of the stuff that you seem to have got from Yorke Barnsley is incredible. All I had was a skateboard! You've been in deep space, you can fly, disappear things, space-time shift, make *QuanTum* and change colour. It was you who gave the world *async*!'

'S'pose,' Mazik admitted, reluctantly, trying hard not to weaken. 'But they're not things I've done by myself. It's just magic; like Yorke put a spell on me.' Mazik sniffed. 'There's a difference, y'know!'

'Well, you're underestimating what you've done. It took great courage to rescue Chepi. Who knows what might have happened to you?' Jimmy held the Ice Cream Parlour door open for Mazik to go in.

'That would be worth something if I'd realised the risk beforehand, but I never even thought about it. So it's worthless.'

'No, you're so wrong. You did it instinctively. A coward would have just walked away. You may not have done a risk assessment, but you knew you had to go on a dangerous mission and you did it without hesitation! Strawberry or vanilla?'

Mazik ordered Sundae Best, the biggest and most expensive item on the menu, watched with relish as it was made up and balanced it carefully to a nearby table. Jimmy joined him. 'Anyway, what about tackling Filthy Scumbag and having the wit and nerve to tie him up?! That was quick-thinking,

heroic and courageous. And, besides, you got back our precious Moon rocks.'

'S'pose,' admitted Mazik, knowing Jimmy's insight was true. But then Mazik froze. He slapped his hand over his forehead. 'I've only just remembered that Yorke sent a message for you!'

'Which was?'

'I'll send a special gift to share with everyone on the big day!'

Mazik was mortified. He'd messed everything up, just when he was winning some recognition. He'd blown it, by his stupidity and forgetfulness.

But Jimmy just laughed at Mazik's obvious discomfort. 'It's *async,*' said Jimmy. 'He sent *async* on our wedding day and you were the medium. The medium is the message. You've done the job perfectly.'

'But it weren't me, Bro!'

'Ah, but it was. You deliberately swallowed *QuanTum* – I'm certain *async* couldn't have spread otherwise – that and a little of *Yorke's spark*, no doubt. You did it on purpose, even if you didn't know what the consequences would be.'

'S'pose,' repeated Mazik.

'Suppose nothing, young man. What you did was magic, Mazik!'

The lump dissolving in Mazik's throat wasn't Sundae Best. 'I've been thinking that all these magic tricks I've got from *Qua* – I call them *Quasies* – are something I should get rid of. I mean, I haven't got enough control. Something awful might happen.'

'You don't need to do that,' frowned Jimmy. 'Look, it's a sibling thing. The young one can be a bit, well, let's say "impulsive".'

'You mean "reckless", don't you?'

'Well, to be honest, yes, I do. But it's not a blame thing. When I was not much older than you are now, Dad was killed and I had to take a lot of responsibility. Mum coped by burying herself in work, so I guess I had to grow up very quickly. Otherwise, I'd have been just like you.'

'You're telling me to grow up!?'

'There's no hurry! See how far you've come, just since my book launch. You're tremendous fun, as you are. Just get control of these, erm, *Quasies* and you'll be fine – perfect!' Jimmy held out his hand for Mazik to shake. 'I couldn't be more proud of you!'

Mazik managed to laugh rather than choke. He grabbed Jimmy's hand enthusiastically, his face glowing with pride. He thrust his other hand deep into his pocket and pulled out a fluff-coated sweet. 'Would you like to finish my gobstopper?'

'That's too a great an honour, Mazik. It's only fair you finish what you started.'

'You mean, the gobstopper?'

'That, too. But what I really mean is that you can't leave Smarmycreep like that. He's suffered enough. You have the *Quasies*. Use them properly and it'll be a rite of passage – from childhood to responsibility. It's a big step. Are you man enough?'

~

Everyone was thrilled and delighted with the amazing transformation wrought by *async*. Everyone, that is, except one, world-famous fashion designer. Spiky Smarmycreep watched the wedding photographer's video repeatedly, on his hospital-room television. He viewed it through his one good eye, as he lay in a miserable turmoil of discomfort and uncertainty.

His bitter resentment grew like a simmering boil. The video showcased Harmony's remarkable *fabar* dress and he knew that nothing he made could possibly compare. To make things worse, he instinctively knew that nobody would want his outrageous clothes, when complexions were now a riot of colour.

Smarmycreep was a man driven by the need to be recognised. He craved celebrity, though notoriety would do just as well. But, most of all, he worshipped money. Were he to fail in any venture, revenge would erupt like an exploding volcano!

His vengeance focussed on a single target – Mazik Spark. That night, the sedatives had no effect. Smarmycreep's mind was working overtime, on a devious scheme to put an end to Mazik's interference – if not an end to Mazik himself.

But Mazik also lay awake, restlessly recalling all the things that Jimmy had said. There was only one thing to do – he resolved to muster all his powers and put the situation right.

Sometime well after midnight, when all was quiet in the hospital, Mazik space-time shifted into Smarmycreep's isolation room and stood at the end of his bed.

Smarmycreep's grossly swollen eye nearly bulged out of the socket. Had he the strength to lift his huge hands, he'd have throttled the intruder. 'What the hell do *you* want, Spark!?' he screamed.

'I want you to calm down and stop screaming,' said Mazik, coolly, keeping just out of reach. 'You'll have nurses running in here to see what's wrong!'

'What *do* you want!?' repeated Smarmycreep hotly. 'Where did you come from?'

Mazik ignored the second question. 'I want a deal.'

'Who are *you* to do a deal, punk?' said Smarmycreep, smirking arrogantly.

'Oh, you can stay like that for the rest of your life, for all I care,' replied Mazik, resolutely.

'Oh yeah and what do you think you can do about it?'

'Think about it,' said Mazik, daringly.

'What's there to think about? What...' Smarmycreep paused. 'What...'

'Go on,' said Mazik teasingly. 'What about the sponge ball?'

'The ball?' repeated Smarmycreep, falteringly, his thoughts derailed. 'The dog ball in my flat... You mean, it was *you* that put it there?'

'Maybe,' replied Mazik knowingly.

'You mean...' he hesitated, frowning, 'picking up that sticky ball caused all this!?' He was about to explode with anger.

'I can help you.'

'Come on, kid!' he laughed, 'The best doctors are completely stumped. What can *you* do?' But a tiny candle of hope for his recovery was flickering through his thoughts and his aggression started to dissolve.

Suddenly, Smarmycreep's enormous nose shrank back to normal. His jaw hung in disbelief.

'What…? How did you do that? What do you mean, *deal*?'

'I'll return you to normal, if you stop hounding me,' said Mazik. 'In fact, you can turn yourself around. Go and do something useful.'

'And if I refuse?' Smarmycreep's nose sprang back to a foot long. Mazik held up his mobile, showing a photograph of a man with a bleeding scar, crouching over a drain. Smarmycreep groaned in defeat, 'Okay, okay. Anything you say, just get me out of this mess and I'll do whatever you want,' he begged.

~

When Smarmycreep awoke after a long sleep, he was again filled with dread fear of his terrible appearance. He opened his eyes and found to his astonishment that his nose was no longer blocking his view. He looked down at his hands and they *weren't* hanging out of the bottom of the bed on elongated arms; they were normal. He gingerly raised a hand and felt his hair. It wasn't the size of a garden shrub any longer. He brushed his hand over his huge bulging eye, but it, too, was now back to normal.

Instead of celebrating, he curled up on his bed and wept bitterly. 'I'm obnoxious and odious! I'm grotesque and repellent!' He recalled a sort of dream vision; surely, it hadn't really happened?

Mazik Spark hadn't *actually* appeared in his room, it was just too absurd! But, either way, his inflated hatred had dissolved along with his monstrous inflammations.

He composed himself, dressed, thanked the staff and left the hospital. He went to the barbers and had a haircut and shave. He bought some plain, practical clothes from a charity shop, called in to see his bank manager, then took the tube to High Woodley. He posted a small packet of the *fabar* ribbon he'd stolen from Harmony's dress through their front door, with a note of apology and more than enough money to repair any damage and harm done.

Then, he knocked on Mazik's front door. Amy opened the door, wearing a dress cut from Grandma Lucy's roll of *fabar*. Spiky was speechless.

Worn by Amy, *fabar* was even more spectacular than when on the cadaverous model, or in the videos – or the slender ribbon he'd held.

Amy was taken aback that he should arrive on their doorstep. 'You're Spiky Smarmycreep! I'm not sure you're welcome here.'

'Oh…er…please…Mrs Spark,' he begged. 'Erm… You look sensational in that dress!'

Amy stepped back. She was shocked and nearly slammed the door shut.

He almost died with embarrassment at such a crass start. 'No! Sorry, what I mean is that's...that's...er...the most beautiful fabric I've ever seen!' He tried not to stare and breathed deeply to recover his composure and gather his thoughts. 'I've come to apologize. What I did was unforgivable, but I've learnt my lesson,' he added, humbly. 'I'm determined to become a reformed character.'

He paused. 'I've bought a bone for Chepi and some football cards for Mazik. You might not believe it, but it's all I can afford, now. I've just given all my money to charity! I'll never cheat again. I'm going to try and find an honest job, now. I wanted to call by and thank you.' He expected her to slam the door in his face, but she accepted the gifts graciously and he continued, 'That is, truly, the most wonderful dress I've ever seen. If you don't mind me asking, where does the material come from?'

As she closed the door, she simply replied:

'Barnsley.'

~

Early the next morning, while Orion still shone brightly overhead, Gramps put on his shorts and the kettle and stepped onto the dewy back lawn, to find a new bundle of lustrous *fabar* and a small heap of *QuanTum* capsules. He looked up wistfully at the star-filled sky and said aloud, 'Cap'n Yorke Barnsley! Tha's electric blue and maybe a bit nesh, wi' right daft name, but tha's a grand lad! Champion! That were best ride of mi life. Sorry our Mazik were pullin' buttons, levers, keys and *thingummyjigs*.'

'As for fabric and compost for fruit and veg? Magic! Ta, muchly, our lad.' He saluted skyward with his flat cap.

Anyone looking closely would have seen a nostalgic twinkle in the old man's eyes.